DARK SHADE
OF EVIL

W. E. PALMER

Bill Palmer

w.e.palmer@outlook.com

First Published: Dec 2021

KDP ISBN: 9798716250284

OTHER BOOKS BY W.E. PALMER

JAB

The Truth Hurts

Below The Belt

CHAPTER 1

A glance at the clock on the bedside table told Ray it was 3.40 a.m. He had woken himself up trying to fight off another demon, sighing heavily the forty year old sat up straight, trying to remember the last time he had enjoyed a full night's kip, he couldn't. Pulling the blanket off of him Ray swung his legs out of the bed and stood up, he stretched his arms skyward and yawned before scratching his bollocks, then wearing just a pair of boxer pants he made his way out of the bedroom and headed for the bathroom because even at this unearthly hour of the day Ray needed a shower, that was when he heard an unfamiliar noise coming from the living room. Ray stopped dead in his tracks and continued to listen while trying not to breathe, he had an unwanted guest, or maybe guests, in the house, he was sure of that. His line of work ensured that Ray never collected his full quota of sleep because ghosts would haunt him relentlessly and he often woke up soaked in sweat and shouting out in anger, tonight had not been an exception. His chosen profession also meant that Ray had to have his wits about him at all times and It was on occasions such as this that he wondered why he had not become a bricklayer or a carpenter. As a lad Ray had excelled in all practical lessons at school and had sat at the top of his class in most subjects until a well-timed left hook had dumped his woodwork teacher firmly on his arse and ensured an end to any further education for him. Ray placed himself tight against the hallway wall and moved closer to the living room door. There was no furniture in the hallway to hinder his progress and the carpet meant he could move quietly but every movement Ray made was done so with an overcautious action making him resemble the cat out of Tom and Jerry trying to sneak up on the mouse.

Ray was unaware of the similarity, which was just as well because a fit of laughter right now would dump him firmly up to his neck in shit if there was an intruder in the flat. The furniture in the living room was sparse, to say the least, comprising of one armchair, one small coffee table and a portable tele that stood on an upside-down beer crate. If somebody was in the lounge, they were not there to rob the place; Ray was certain of that. "Come on, hurry up and open the door for fuck's sake." Ray had played the waiting game on many an occasion but had never enjoyed it even though he had been told more than once that patience was a virtue. Had the intruder heard Ray? Believing he was the only one in the apartment, he hadn't been quiet up until he had heard that noise; after all, there was no reason to be when you lived on your own. If the intruder had heard Ray, then this had most certainly turned in to one of those cat and mouse games. Unarmed, Ray had no intention of going into the lounge and possibly facing somebody with a gun; he wasn't bulletproof after all, so he perched himself by the door and listened carefully for any sort of sound of movement from his unwelcome visitor. He stood there for what seemed a lifetime and heard nothing, his concentration level was being tested to the extreme, and he failed the exam when he started to think about the events of the day before. Ray, armed with a baseball bat and with two accomplices, had paid a man charged with rape a visit and meted out a large portion of retribution. It was the first time that Ray had not worked on his own and had been employed just to give somebody a beating; he was a hitman and used to taking out his target, removing them from the planet. He remembered the sound of bones breaking under the force of the bat, and the horrified screams that had left his victim's mouth after each of the blows that he had delivered with ferocity had landed on target and even under these circumstances that he found himself in it caused him to smile, the screams had only fuelled Ray's anger and caused him to reign down more blows with every ounce of his strength that he could muster. He did not stop when the screams did either; one of his workmates, who had not had to raise a finger up until now, had grabbed hold of Ray's arm and brought him back to the now. "You'll kill the poor bastard with a few more blows, time to stop. The order wasn't to finish him. You're supposed to keep him alive so that he suffers for his crime." Ray stopped the downward movement of the baseball bat in mid-air and moved out of the killing zone.

"Yeah, you're right, sorry about that I got a bit carried away."

Ray lowered his arm and then delivered a vicious kick into his victim's bollocks. No sound came out of the beaten, helpless rapist, and that caused Ray to laugh at his victory before he turned and walked away, followed closely by the other two who had exchanged a look of disbelief and a shake of their heads behind Ray's back before closing the door on the property and the victim. The three men walked at a fast pace for several blocks as they returned to their car that had been parked a safe distance away. Ray had placed the baseball bat in a specially made pocket on the inside of his jacket. "You're one crazy mother fucker Ray."

"Fuck me, he's right, Ray."

The look Ray returned to the two of them made it clear their comments were not appreciated. The drive that followed had been made in total silence. Ray also remembered counting out the thick wad of £50 notes he had received for services rendered and realised he could never earn that sort of money as a builder. It brought a smile to his normally sober face, which soon vanished as he was brought back to the present by a creaking noise as the handle of the door was slowly being forced down. He wouldn't be getting paid for tonight's work, but he would hopefully enjoy it just the same. Who the fuck was this in his flat, he had worked hard to make sure that nobody knew his real name or address, and if the intruder was a burglar, he would have left the way he had entered when he realised there was nothing to nick. Somebody wanted him taken care of, and he was pretty sure that he knew who that person was; he wouldn't have long to wait now before he could confirm his suspicions.

The handle continued to be moved down for what seemed like an eternity, and then the door slowly opened into the room. Ray kept very still and waited. Right now, he held the upper hand because he knew where his enemy was. He continued to wait, still scared to breathe, everything was moving in slow motion, something he was not used to and then a head appeared and looked up the passageway; before it had turned in his direction, Ray moved forward and struck a punch to the intruder's temple. The adversary collapsed to the floor, poleaxed by the single blow, and things had once again returned to normal speed. Ray moved into the room and knelt down by the victim, rolling the body on to its back; he pulled up the black balaclava that was hiding the intruder's face, and it confirmed his suspicions. Ray pulled the balaclava back down and then delivered two more heavy blows to the person's face before making his way to the kitchen, where he took out a roll of tape and a length of clothesline from the cupboard under the sink before returning to the still prone body that filled the doorway.

With a great amount of effort, the body was lifted on to the armchair and tied up before a piece of sticky tape was placed over the mouth, and the balaclava once again pulled down to hide his attacker's face. Then, just because he could, he delivered a couple of sickening blows to his intruder's body. The cracking sounds that accompanied the blows told Ray that he had broken ribs. Feeling pleased, he then delivered another blow to the side of the head with such force that both chair and body crashed sideways to the floor. Ray grabbed the chair to right it, but the effort was too much, and so he let it go before walking to his bedroom and getting dressed; Ray then packed his belongings into a holdall along with the large amount of cash he had in a bag before attaching the silencer to his gun and returning to the trussed, unconscious intruder where he buried two bullets in his head, the blood leaked through the balaclava and pooled on the floor under the head and beyond, making a mess of the room and causing another smile to spread across Ray's face, the hitman then walked out of the apartment and on to an empty street, he would be needing to find himself a new address now.

Ray inhaled and swallowed a large amount of the early morning freshness before pulling his grey duffle coat hood over his head. Looking all around several times, Ray was happy to believe that he was alone, and so he set off for the train station at a brisk pace. The hitman needed to put a fair distance between his current location and himself while he decided what to do about the predicament he now found himself in. Ray knew the identity of his wanna-be assassin; he also knew who had sent him, and he needed to deal with that person before he could move on with his life; the woman responsible wanted him dead, but he had developed feelings for her and was reluctant to end her life; however he did not intend spending the time he had left on the planet having to keep moving and looking over his shoulder.

CHAPTER 2

Robert Smith entered the world on a grey, cold and wet Friday morning. His mother was not too pleased with the day that he chose; it meant she couldn't go out on the piss for the weekend, and the father, well, he'd had it on his toes as soon as Kath had told him he'd knocked her up.

"He'd have been a useless father anyway". Kath had told her parents.

They both lifted their eyes skyward and tutted simultaneously before walking off in disbelief. This would be their third grandchild born out of wedlock, and to make matters worse, the third father that had not hung around or put his hand in his pocket for the kid's upkeep.

"The problem with Kath is the drinking, she gets pissed and it loosens her knicker elastic."

Mum nodded in agreement.

"How's she gonna raise three kids on her own?" she had replied.

"It's a bloody drain on our savings, Mother, and nobody in their right mind will wanna marry her now so it's gonna keep costing us, she needs sterilising or a chastity belt fitting." Kath's Dad let out a long staccato sigh.

" Why doesn't she go on the pill? I don't understand how she lands up pregnant three times, once is one time too many, shit happens to us all but three times, well there's

6

no excuse for that. Never even thought about an abortion either." Mum's face wore a sad expression.

Nine months later, they both tutted in unison before donning their coats, leaving their home and making their way to the hospital armed with flowers and chocolates.

CHAPTER 3

Robert and his two siblings that were two and four years older than him, had been brought up the hard way. The three of them had needed to grow up fast and to fend for themselves because their mother had left them to their own devices on so many occasions, even worse was the fact that she had needed her money for the pub, so even a proper meal was a luxury for her three offspring. Lizzie was the middle child and John the eldest. Other kids in the area had all grown up with both parents, celebrated birthdays with parties and Christmas with families. Not these three though, and as a result, they had no friends; they grew up just knowing each other. Never receiving an invite to classmates birthday parties or being invited around their houses after school. The parents of the other children had not wanted their offspring anywhere near these three little bastards. John, being the eldest, had experienced the resentment towards the family first. He had come home from school crying because of the names he had been called, and his mother had clumped him hard around the earhole so that he had something to cry for. After that one time, the tears stopped, and he also stopped telling his mother about the name-calling or how he had to sit alone at playtime. When school finished on a Friday, John had wanted to feel relieved to have two days away from the solitude he experienced every weekday, but it never happened that way; instead, he hated the weekends more. Although only five, he was left looking after his sister and little brother while mum went drinking. Robert would be put to bed by his mum but often woke up, and John did not know what to do to stop his brother crying; he didn't have a clue how to console him, so closed the bedroom door and ignored the noise.

Lizzie had been three and wanted her brother to play games like hide and seek, but she had also started crying when she could not find her big brother. John had let himself out the front door of the maisonette where they lived and sat on the top stair of the stairwell, hunched up against the wall.

When mum returned from the pub, she would be drunk and accompanied by a man who was equally inebriated. Kath would clump John around the ear and order him indoors, where he would be sent to the bedroom that he shared with the other two children. He would lay on his bed and listen to the grunts, groans and screams of pleasure that accompanied his mother's shag.

When he got up in the morning, his mother was always asleep, alone and naked. John was eight years old when he met Alan. Alan was a gang member and also the first person to show him any sort of attention. He had sat next to him on the staircase and made general chit-chat. John liked Alan; nobody else did. The seventeen-year-old was a thug with a ruthless streak way beyond his years. The teenager had been dragged up the hard way but did not blame his father for the way he had treated him even though the bastard had beaten him on many occasions, he had even put his cigarettes out on him, and he had the scars to prove that but that had been the way things were for him and he'd grown up not knowing anything different. His mother had divorced the sadistic bastard when he had turned his attention toward her and started knocking her about as well; she had always turned a blind eye to the way he had treated Alan but had no intentions of suffering the same fate. His mum had then moved the new boyfriend in just a couple of weeks later before marrying him because she had needed security in her life; it was not easy being an unmarried mum, and most people had shunned her for tolerating her first husband's antics for so long. A finger of disapproval had been pointed in her direction on more than one occasion, " That's her, the bitch let her ol' man knock their son about ya know, he's turned up at school battered and bruised more times than you've had hot dinners I dare say." Tuts of disapproval had been sent in her direction.

When his mum had met Patrick and then got hitched, Alan was happy for her, but Patrick had never liked Alan and did not want him around; unfortunately for Alan, he took to beating him as well, his mum chose to turn a blind eye again, but the evidence of the beatings were there in the form of further scars that he carried around on his body. Alan was happy for his mum but could not continue to live under the same roof as Patrick any more. He had been fifteen years old when he moved out, and living rough had not been easy, but the teenager had handled it well, and now, after two years on the street, nobody fucked with him any more. Alan had learned to mete out punishment to anyone who tried to mess with him. One bastard had tried to shag him when he was sixteen; he had cut his cock off and shoved it down his throat. Word soon spread, and none of the other homeless community wanted the aggro attached to messing with him, so he was left alone. He was only a kid in most people's eyes, but Alan had become notorious because of his evil streak.

CHAPTER 4

'Big H', who for some strange reason was somewhat short in stature, was told about Alan and took him under his wing. He gave the youngster a roof over his head and three meals a day. "I've landed on me feet 'ere", Alan had thought, but of course, he had to pay for the kindness shown to him by 'Big H'. To start with, Alan had accompanied other lads that the modern-day Fagin had taken under his wing on robberies. Alan had been a fast learner and before long was leading a gang. Some of the robberies had been carried out in houses with people in them, and Alan had shown a fondness in beating badly anyone who had tried to defend what was rightfully theirs.

Alan had called around to see John most evenings, and John had looked forward to his company to the point where he became angry when he did not show; he took that anger out on his two younger siblings, who soon began to hate their big brother. They had cried and begged their mum not to leave them alone with John, but their mum's love for alcohol and sex was far stronger than her love for them, and their pleas had fallen on deaf ears.

Lizzie and Robert had both been left feeling happy when Alan had taken John away from them because they had both suffered enough beatings from the sadistic little bastard, and it was like God had answered their prayers when he left. Mum had not even noticed that John had gone for several weeks. Her parents had called around and asked their daughter where her son was.

"He must be out with his mates." She had replied.

"He doesn't have any." The reply was made in unison.

"John doesn't live here anymore, Grandad." Lizzie had chipped in, "he went off with that other boy weeks ago." Bloody hell, he did have a friend, so who's been looking after you and Robert?"

"We don't need anyone Grandad and it's better without John cos he used to hit us."

Grandad had tried to make his daughter take some responsibility for her children, but all his pep talks and all her promises had vanished in to thin air when her need for alcohol rose to the top of her list of priorities once again.

It was with a heavy heart that Grandad had reported his daughter to the Social Services and had Lizzie and Robert taken into care.

"It's for the best", his wife had told him, and although he knew that was true, it still hurt him to snitch on his own.

Lizzie and Robert had been separated and fostered out. Mum erased all three children from her memory with the help of more alcohol and more one night stands.

CHAPTER 5

Alan had taken John away from the misery of his home life and given him the comfort of a clean bed, three regular meals a day and new clothes. John was more than happy to pay Alan back for the kindness he had shown him because nobody had ever been this nice to him before.

He was posted through little windows of the houses they robbed and would then made his way to the front door and open it for Alan and his mates. Alan would smile at John and pat his head, and John then knew that he had done well.

'Big H' was very happy with the new partnership and the bounties that Alan and John brought him, and so he took extra care of both the boys.

Nine fruitful years passed without a hitch. 'Big H' grew richer, and Alan and John wanted for nothing; all was good in the house. Their special treatment caused some friction with the other lads that also lived under Big H's wing, and a couple of them had tried to topple the pair from their top spot; they had been dealt with viciously. Their incomplete torsos had been shown to all the other members of the gang. They made poor imitations of the Venus de Milo, and the message not to fuck with these two had been received by all.

At 17 and 26 years of age, Alan and John believed they were untouchable. They had literally gotten away with murder on several occasions. Both the boys had taken a liking to a drink, but neither of them had ever been drunk. They kept their wits about them at all times. They had both lost their cherries to prostitutes, and both enjoyed sex, but there were no girlfriends to be seen because neither of them needed the extra baggage that a relationship brought with it.

One poor soul had been heard to say that the pair were gay because of their close bond to one another. His tongue had been cut out as a punishment for his crime, minus the anaesthetic, before being shot and his body dumped in some footings for a new bridge.

The deadly duo were riding high on the crest of a very big wave when they were summoned by the boss and promoted from burglary to protection. Their ruthless streaks and love of violence made them naturals for the promotion, and their notoriety continued to gain momentum.

CHAPTER 6

Robert's young life had been bereft of any form of love. His mother had never shown him any affection, and his grandparents had let it be known to him that his existence was the result of a drunken fuck his mother had given in exchange for the alcohol that her one night stand had bought her and that he along with his two siblings were an expense that they could do without. Lizzie had been the one to look out for him, unlike his brother, and they had a bond that had been broken when he had been taken into care at the tender age of four. Fostered out to so many families, Robert had struggled and, in fact, been unable to return any kindness shown to him and had not fitted in with any of them. His home address changed frequently, and so did his school. The beatings John had dished out had hurt, but the bruises he received healed; however, the mental damage left scars that were deep and would not. Robert was growing up alone without anyone to call a friend.

The lad had hated school and never made any friends there. He was never at any school long enough to make lasting relationships anyway, and his ignorance of love and inability to socialise had led him into many scrapes. He had lost a few of them early on, but a vicious streak emerged in him as well, and on more than one occasion, an adult had been needed to peel him off his hapless victim. Robert was becoming one mean bastard when he walked out of his latest foster home and chose to live on the streets at the tender age of 13; unfazed by the move, he was a match for anyone who tried it on with him despite his lack of years, his short life had been a hard one, and as a result, he had become one tough bastard.

Robert had survived for two years on the streets but wanted more from life; he intended to start climbing the rungs on life's social ladder. He had become a very good pickpocket, and with his ill-gotten gains, he managed to eat well and dress smartly. There had been a big boost of good fortune for him when he had walked off with a holdall somebody had put down and turned away from. The split second that the bag had been left unattended had proven to be long enough for the light-fingered little toe rag to grab it and have it on his toes. He was soon lost in the crowd, and one frantic previous owner of the holdall was left pirouetting in that same crowd in an attempt to recapture what was rightfully his. He failed, and his loss had proven to be Robert's large-sized gain. The bag was stuffed with money and jewellery. Robert felt no guilt for the crime he'd committed as he believed he had stolen from a fellow thief.

With the money already in the bag added to the cash he made flogging the 'Tom', Robert had enough to buy some fake ID and then rent a furnished apartment. His life on the streets was over, and at 15 years of age, he was starting to climb that social ladder just like he had planned. His new ID said he was 19 years old.

When he wasn't on the rob, the young upstart began people watching, realising he needed social skills to keep climbing that ladder of his. Robert was a quick learner and made the climb two rungs at a time.

By the time Robert was actually 19 years old, he was moving around in some nice circles. The youngster cut a dapper figure in his three-piece suits, shirts and ties and started being seen with some decent bits of skirt hanging on his arm.

He wined, dined, shagged and robbed them all. He made sure that every single one of them were married women and therefore unlikely to expose their loss because of their infidelity.

One woman stepped out of line and came clean to her 'ol man about what she'd been up to. Enraged by the confession, the geezer had slapped his missus and then gone in search of Robert to take back the money he'd nicked and teach him a lesson. It proved to be a big mistake, and the beating he took for his troubles left him concussed, crippled and close to death.

What had been a life-changing day for the husband had been just another day and another problem solved for Robert.

CHAPTER 7

Lizzie found herself in a foster home aged just six but had loved the attention she was given by her part-time parents, who had made her feel wanted. Lizzie's previous life soon became a bad dream that these nice people had helped her to forget. Regular meals, nice clothes and new friends at school made Lizzie feel like a queen, and when she was finally adopted by that family, the young lady believed all her Christmases and birthdays had arrived at once.

Her new dad had sat her on his knee and bounced her up and down, tickled her and made her laugh and chased her around the living room pretending to be a monster. When Lizzie was left alone with this man, that pretence became the real thing. The tickling became more intimate, as did the kisses and cuddles. Lizzie was 10 years old when her adopted dad introduced her to an erection and abused her. The poor thing believed the bastard when he told her he was showing her a special love that had to be kept a secret just between the two of them.

The first time he had entered her, she had cried out in pain, but daddy had held her close and kissed her better. Lizzie had survived and gone on to enjoy her special attention. She would keep their secret safe and continue to enjoy their intimate relationship because, at last, Lizzie's life had meaning; she was finally a loved member of a family, she finally belonged.

Whenever Mum went out and Lizzie was left alone with Dad, the youngster felt a happy glow. She knew that she was about to receive some special attention from him. Then one day, a couple of Uncles arrived, and Lizzie was allowed to share her special love with them too. How special was she to receive all this love from three men, and the Uncles even gave her money and presents in return for her attentions.

Lizzie was 14 years old when she brought her best friend home from school. She had asked her Mum if Jenny could come round for tea.

"Of course she can Lizzie, it is so lovely that you have a special friend."

The tea her adopted mother made was memorable with a dessert and bottles of pop, and Jenny wanted Lizzie to go to her house the next week so that she could do the same for her new best friend, the friendship blossomed as a result of those two teas, and they became a regular occurrence. The two girls became inseparable both at school and after.

Lizzie thought that she was a very lucky girl with the special secret love she shared with her dad and two uncles, plus she now had a best friend that she spent a lot of happy hours with.

Her happiness continued for the best part of two years before everything went belly up, and the poor girl found herself back in care.

Her best friend Jenny had ruined her life, and suddenly Lizzie hated her. The two girls had been in Jenny's bedroom talking about a boy that Jenny fancied. Jenny had told her how she wanted to kiss him and maybe go further than just a kiss and had been shocked when Lizzie asked how her dad would feel about her 'doing it' with somebody else.

"Somebody else Lizzie, what do you mean?"

"Are you not your Daddy's special girl?"

When Lizzie had confessed her secret to her best friend, she thought she would keep it a secret too because Lizzie believed that Jenny was her daddy's special little girl, but to her dismay, she had found out that Jenny wasn't and her best friend had been shocked by Lizzie's news and told her that her dad and two uncles were wrong to do what he had to her. Lizzie accused her of being jealous of her special relationship, and the friends then had their first argument; Lizzie had slapped Jenny before bursting in to tears and running home, where she threw herself on top of her bed and sobbed in to her pillow.

The next couple of days saw Lizzie's world come crashing down around her. Police and Social Workers had invaded her life and taken her away from the people she believed loved her. Lizzie was 16 years old and alone again. She hated Jenny and wished she had never told her about the secret. There was nobody to make her feel special now. Instead, she had people telling her how she had been wronged and feeling sorry for her. She was told that she had been abused and what she had done had been wrong.

Lizzie struggled to understand what she was being told and cried for what seemed like forever to her.

The poor girl had to live in a home now where she slept in a dormitory and shared a table and television with other kids like her. She had lost her mum and dad and their love; they had been replaced by carers that caused her so much unhappiness; the poor girl had fallen from her social tree and landed with a thud on some very hard ground.

Lizzie's head had been messed with, and at 16, she was struggling to cope with all that was happening. The social misfit decided that she did not want to stay where she was for too long. She was fed up with the questioning from everybody and did not like telling them about her secrets that she had shared with her dad. Why were they recording everything she said? Then she realised she had dropped her dad in the shit right up to his neck. Was that how you repaid people that showed you so much, love?

Lizzie walked out of the home one day and met a woman at the bottom of the path.

"Not more bloody questioning, please." She thought. The woman said Hello to Lizzie and asked her if she fancied some breakfast. A treat for her, and she assured the young girl that would be no nasty questions afterwards, but she did have an offer that would put a smile back on the young girls face. Lizzie went with the woman and ten minutes later was sitting in the café with Claire, that was the name the woman used to introduce herself to the 16-year-old, tucking into a full English.

When they had finished breakfast, Claire took Lizzie for a walk.

"I can get you away from all this shit if you want me to Lizzie." Claire had told her.

Lizzie liked the sound of the offer and decided to move into Claire's house with her; it was a two-hour drive to her new address.

"You can have proper meals Lizzie, your own bedroom and want for nothing," Claire told her, "but you have to keep a few men happy in return."

"Just like I did my dad and uncles?" Lizzie asked.

"Yes Lizzie, just like that. You make the men happy and that will please me and then I will look after you."

"Oh, fuck! Lizzie thought, "here we go again." But her own room with a TV and record player and no more questions from Social workers and Police sounded good to her.

"Oh! One more thing Lizzie, you mustn't leave the house for a while."

"Deal," said Lizzie "I'll have all I need right there in my room."

CHAPTER 8

John never looked back; why would he? There was nothing worth looking back at, but the forward vision that he was filled with saw a future that was full of promise; with Alan by his side, the view straight ahead was looking proper rosy for him.

The pair kept 'Big H' very happy with their work, and he kept their stomachs and wardrobes full for them. He owned a healthy wallet too because John was paid good money to inflict pain and misery on others, and for some reason, he enjoyed his job immensely. He was a cruel, sadistic bastard but a very happy, cruel, sadistic bastard.

When he and Alan entered people's premises to collect 'Big H's' money, they were paid in full, even when it nearly crippled the people's livelihood. Their reputation went before them, and nobody wanted to upset the duo.

When a rival gang had tried to muscle in on their business, 'Big H' had said just two words to them – "Sort it."

The pair did not need telling twice. With a savagery beyond compare, they dismembered the bodies of the people that upset them, and when the police had arrived at the scene, several had thrown up at the sight that met them.

One business that they collected protection money from had fronted the pair out and told them they no longer needed their services; the business had been razed to the ground.

'Big H' put his money about and paid the 'old bill' a sizeable amount of money so that John and Alan never had to answer for any of the crimes they committed.

The pair of them were sitting in a boozer one day having a pint and a chat about nothing really when Alan asked why they needed 'Big H'. They could earn more, he said, if they ruled him out of the equation.

"Dodgy ground I think, Alan, and to be honest with you I'm happy with the way thing things are."

"Just think about it John, that's all."

As they finished their pint and chat, a bloke sitting near them got up and walked out, his walk was with a purpose, and he was wearing an ear to ear grin. Now, when people tell stories, they sometimes wander a little from the truth or omit bits, and when this bloke reported back to 'Big H', he forgot to mention that John was not keen on the idea. He dropped both Alan and John straight in the shit.

"Silly bastards," Big H had said, "everything was going so well and now they have to be dealt with and replaced." It was with a heavy heart that he picked up the phone and made the call, and when he replaced the receiver, he let out a sad and heavy sigh.

CHAPTER 9

Ray put the receiver back on its cradle and rubbed his hands together. A new contract had just landed in his lap with a big payday attached. He collected a few bits together and threw them in his rucksack; Nylon cord, sticky tape, a couple of socks to use as gags, a pair of pliers, a two and a half-pound club hammer, along with a balaclava, a black tracksuit and a pair of black leather gloves, he also packed his gun and silencer along with his set of knuckle dusters. He double-locked the door to the apartment on his way out and walked the couple of blocks to where he parked his car, a very unassuming white VW Polo. Ray placed the rucksack in the boot and then climbed in behind the wheel. He started the engine and drove off, destination – the office of his employer where he would be given all the necessary paperwork for his job. The next few days would see him stopping in a few B and Bs under an alias. There was nothing about Ray that made him stand out from the crowd. Ray was a Mister Average, just the way he liked it. So average in fact that his employer had wondered if he was capable of fulfilling his contract. "Never judge a book by its cover," he told himself with a reasonable conviction, and anyway, if Ray didn't deliver this time, the boss would not have to pay the balance due, Big H really should have had no reason to doubt Ray's abilities seeing as he'd delivered on all his previous contracts.

Ray had laughed once again inwardly when he met Big H, remembering the first time that he had introduced himself. 'Fat Harry' might have suited him better. "But who gives a fuck what he looks like really or what he calls himself," he told himself, "he's parting with a lot of money to sort this problem."

A little bit of research and following the two blokes he had to take care of told him that this contract was likely to be one of the toughest he had accepted. He had witnessed their capabilities and was impressed by their ferocity, "I've got my work cut out here for fuck's sake", he told himself, "I need to split the pair up to take care of them one at a time and no fucking about capturing and torturing them either."

Three days into following the pair, Ray got the break he needed when a woman, who introduced herself to the pair as Claire, had taken Alan away to meet a girl that worked for her. John had laughed at the interest Alan had shown for someone he had not met before. "You can pick from any number of birds all waiting to be shagged by you, so why this one?"

"Claire tells me she's something special and so I'm keen to find out why, I'll catch up with you tomorrow John." Alan walked out of the pub with Claire holding on to his arm; John had been left alone. Ray was a happy man, he just needed to be patient a little while longer, and half of the contract would be complete. A pint and a whisky chaser later, his patience was rewarded again when John needed to visit the gents and take a piss. Once his target had entered the gents, Ray waited long enough for him to be halfway through his piss before he followed him in, taking his Glock G2B out of his pocket and fitting the silencer to it before entering. One pull of the trigger later, Ray walked back into the bar and finished his drink before leaving. John was slumped over the urinal, his head resting in the bowl minus its brain that was splattered up the wall. Ray made his way to his motor and drove to Alan's address, where he parked up and waited to complete the job.

CHAPTER 10

Claire introduced Alan to Lizzie; he'd seen better-looking birds and ones with nicer figures to be honest, but when he left the house quite a few quid lighter than when he'd entered he had no complaints with the time he'd spent in the girl's company, she had more than delivered. It was to be the last shag he would have because half an hour later, he suffered the same fate as his partner in crime; his body was left face down on the pavement outside his gaff. Ray went to collect his payment from Big H, who handed over the balance with the same heavy heart he'd had when he had given the contract to the hitman, "take the pair out," he'd told Ray, and as a result, he'd just lost his best two workers, adding insult to injury Ray had turned down his offer of full-time work. It took several shots of single malt for the boss to recover, but he did. "I can replace them easy enough," he told himself, but he wasn't convinced by the statement.

Ray drove back to his new address, quids in and with the kit he had taken with him untouched. He hadn't expected the job to be that easy, and he laughed again when he thought of 'Big H'. "Who the fuck gave the little fat geezer that name." His previous employer had been a big bloke standing 6'4" tall and weighing in at eighteen and a half stone; the 'BIG' tag would have been better suited to him.

Chapter 11

Robert loved his new lifestyle; there was nothing not to love about it. Nice clothes, gorgeous women, a very healthy bank account and a nice pad. What could go wrong? He looked back on his life, and it made him happy to be where he was. He had achieved a lot, all things considered, but he had no family to love or reciprocate those feelings and sometimes he felt lonely. His mother had been devoid of any feelings; his nan and grandad had tried to show affection but failed; he'd never really connected with his grandparents because of the conversations he had listened to between them and the woman that had brought him into the world, they continually pecked away at her for having given birth to three bastards without one of the blokes that had knocked her up sticking around. He had been made to feel like a burden most of the time, and his big brother John had been an absolute bastard after Alan had shown up. The closest he'd got to any form of love had been with his sister Lizzie. "I wonder where she is now?" he smiled and then dismissed his sibling from his thoughts. Leaning forward in his chair, Robert picked up his straw and sniffed up the line of white powder that lay on the table. This shit made him feel invincible as well as happy. "What a place to be," he thought; he'd just found an extra helping of happiness that would last for the next 15 to 30 minutes. He laid back in his chair and prepared for the forthcoming ride. Afterwards, feeling on top of the world, he took a walk to one of his local boozers in search of his next female victim; he had two in mind.

Brenda was a cute little thing with a cracking figure, and she wore skirts and dresses that stopped just below her arse; she drew attention from a lot of men, Robert had just become the latest one, and when he saw her standing near the bar he looked straight at her, he winked and smiled, and the smile that he received in return told him he was in with a chance. The big 'but' however, was the size of the goon she was married to. His reputation for being a hard nut fitted well with his looks. He sported a busted beak that was plastered across a kisser that hardly ever smiled, and his dark eyes carried a menace that unnerved most men around him. Tonight, however, there was one exception to that rule, fuelled by one too many beers the idiot walked over to where Ron was standing with Brenda just after Robert had arrived and commented on Ron's beak, "Oi Mate, that's a roman nose if ever I saw one." Brenda's ol' man gave him an enquiring look as he delivered the punch line, "It's roman all over ya fuckin' face!"

The laughter that went with the quip was short-lived as Ron's right fist, the size of a sledgehammer, slammed into his face. Ron looked down at the poleaxed comedian, whose face was now covered in claret, and growled before he let out a menacing laugh that accompanied his gruff-voiced comment. "You're on the way to having one yerself now you fuckin' mug!"

The incident had just happened in a crowded boozer that had two bouncers on the door. Everybody had diverted their attentions away from the episode and made themselves busy with idle chit-chat. The doormen came over and picked up the wannabe stand up and carried him out; neither of them looked at Ron. Robert had turned his attentions back to Brenda while Ron was busy, and he passed her another smile that was accompanied by a wink, the return smile came with a blown kiss that confirmed Robert's thoughts that he was in with a shout. "God, I'm gonna enjoy fucking this one", he blew a kiss back as Ron grabbed hold of his missus and made his way to the bar, where he pushed his way to the front and ordered two drinks, after what had just happened and with his size and reputation nobody in the bar had the guts to get upset with him when the barman gave him priority treatment.

Ron was the right-hand man to a weaselly little geezer with dealings in drugs, prostitution and fencing stolen goods. The geezer, who resembled Fagin from Charles Dickens's Oliver Twist and was also called Robert, had once caught one of his workers thieving off him; he had personally removed three of his fingers from his right hand with bolt croppers. Ron had held the poor sod in a vice-like grip while the operation was carried out, there had been no anaesthetic, and the noise that had accompanied each amputation had been loud, to say the least. Robert had just clapped eyes on his namesake's missus and added her to his list of conquests along with Brenda." She should be an easy pull," the young stallion had told himself. It was rumoured that her ol' man neglected her because he preferred young boys. However, both the boss and his heavy proudly wore their other halves on their arms and paraded them like trophies so they wouldn't take kindly to somebody else fucking them, and both women should pay handsomely to keep their naughty bit of pleasure a secret. Robert looked forward to two decent fucks and then the financial rewards that would follow.

CHAPTER 12

When Alan had been introduced to Lizzie, she thought she recognised the face but couldn't place it. She put it to the back of her mind and concentrated on giving him pleasure; she would deliver value for money, she always did, her 'Dad' had been a good teacher and her a willing pupil. It was several days later when the 'Eureka' moment arrived. "Fuckin' Hell, that was Alan, the bastard that took my brother away."

She now wished she had bitten hard into his cock and see him hurting like they had after he'd arrived on the scene, "You caused me and Robert a lot of pain, I wish I'd given you some back."

Lizzie intended to find out where Claire had met him and then go and seek revenge. She wasn't sure how she'd deal with him yet, but something would come to mind, she was certain.

Claire hadn't been too willing to pass the information to Lizzie but promised her that she would bring Alan back for another session. "Don't go getting feelings for this bloke, Lizzie, will you, cos that'd fuck up everything we've got 'ere at the moment."

"I won't do that Claire, I promise but he had the biggest cock I've ever seen and I fancy a bit more of it. Why would I wanna leave 'ere? I love my job and you Claire."

"Leave it with me Lizzie."

Lizzie went to her room and threw herself on to her bed; she thought about her revenge and laughed as she heard Alan cry out in pain. "I never thought I'd get this chance," she laughed again and then got up and switched her tele on, "I might just get a knife and stab the bastard as well." Lizzie looked forward to meeting Alan again.

CHAPTER 13

It was time for Robert to get inside Brenda's knickers and the thought of the little cracker on the end of his cock filled him with want. It was Friday night, and she would definitely be in the pub with her ol' man. All booted and suited, he splashed a bit of aftershave on, smoothed his hair and smiled at the image in the mirror. "You smooth looking fucker,"' Robert blew a kiss to himself, "operation Brenda here I come."

When he entered the pub, Robert stood for a moment and had a quick shifty round before noticing his prey with her ol' man, the Fagin look-a-like, and his Missus were with them. Robert straightened his tie, smoothed his hair again and then walked purposefully forward to the bar where he pushed his way in between Brenda and a bird that was standing by her side; the woman gave him a cold look that was accompanied by a loud tut. Robert repaid the gestures with a smile and waved at the barman; he ordered himself a whisky, single malt, on the rocks and then turned to his left. Ron and Fagin were busy chatting, and Fagin's Mrs was on the other side to them, looking bored. Brenda had noticed Robert, and as he turned his attentions towards her, she smiled and winked at him. Robert felt a bit of movement inside his pants and smiled back. The barman caused a slight break to his flirting with a 'Sir' followed by an attention seeking cough, Robert took his drink and parted with his cash and then continued with his pursuit of Brenda, he was rewarded with another smile and wink, there was more movement in his pants, and he dropped his right hand down and gave his cock a squeeze. Brenda's eyes followed his hand, and the sight caused her to let a little giggle escape. Ron turned his attention towards his Mrs and Robert looked away.

"Wanna share the joke with us all Brenda?"

His Mrs looked up at him; the smile she'd worn for Robert had left her face, "There is no joke Ron, can I have another drink please?"

Her ol' man turned towards the barman "Oi, four more drinks 'ere."

"Straight away Sir."

The barman stopped serving the customer he was with and started pouring Ron's drinks. The big geezer loved the attention he commanded, and when he passed his Mrs her drink, he made her say thank you. Brenda duly obliged, and her ol' man's chest puffed out; he was a happy man as he turned away from his Missus and gave his attention back to his boss. Brenda turned her back to Robert; dropping her hand down by her side, she moved it across his body and gave his erection a little squeeze through his trousers, winking again before lifting her eyebrows in a teasing manner.

"This one's in the bag," Robert told himself, and he removed a card with his phone number and address on it from his pocket. Passing it discreetly to Brenda, he lifted his glass to his lips and finished his drink. Turning away from the bar, the two exchanged smiles, and Robert made his way out.

"Mission accomplished my friend."

Robert left the pub and jumped into a cab, "In to town please mate."

The driver pulled away from the kerb, and Robert sat

back in the seat, one happy man.

The next day Robert hung around the house, but Brenda never phoned.

"What's she fuckin' playing at, not ringing, I'd have given a pound to a pinch of shit that she'd have rung by now." The young stud was not happy; the situation worsened when she never got in touch the next day. "Something's wrong; she was up for it the other night," he looked in the mirror and studied his image for a moment; you've still got it, son," he said out loud to himself and then blew a kiss. "Right, let's get down to the newsagents and buy a paper, then go to the bookies; if the bitch rings, she'll have to try again later."

Robert opened his front door and stepped out on to the street. He felt the excruciating pain as a punch splattered his beak across his kisser and his knees buckled under the impact; a second punch sent him scurrying into the land of nod. What happened between that and him being woken up by a bucket of cold water being poured over his head was a mystery, but when he did open his minces he was not familiar with his surroundings; he tried to stand up but couldn't. Whoever had kidnapped him had also tied him to a chair. It took a while longer before he realised he was bollock naked.

"Oh fuck! I think I'm in the shit 'ere."

When Ron appeared in front of him with Brenda hanging on the end of his right hand and not looking too comfortable, his thoughts were confirmed. The big fella dropped her in a heap in front of the chair; Brenda looked up at Robert and mouthed a sorry; her features had also been damaged by Ron's fists.

"Right you little bastard, fancy fucking my Mrs do ya? Stand up Brenda and take your coat off."

The woman stood up and undid the buttons to the fur coat she was wearing and let it drop to the floor; she wasn't wearing anything else, and Robert took in the view, everything was as good as he had thought it would be, and he couldn't help but smile.

"Dance for him Brenda, go on start fuckin' dancing."

On order, the woman started to sway her hips and then cupped her tits in her hands, Robert was mesmerised, and his cock stood to attention. Brenda looked at Robert and then looked down at his erection before closing her eyes; Robert closed his too and then felt a sharp pain that caused him to squeal like a stuck pig; he opened his eyes and watched as the big geezer cut off his cock and let it drop to the floor, Robert continued to look down at his blood-covered crutch, his screams had been muted by the pain and he started to heave, his sick exited his body and mixed with the blood. Robert looked on in horror as Ron then took the lid off a can of petrol and dowsed him in it. The less than happy husband's face was suddenly inches from his; the big bastard had hold of Robert's hair and pulled the poor sod's head up with force. The young stud looked into his eyes; they seemed huge and were laughing at him as his executioner pulled out a lighter from his pocket and lit it, letting go of Robert Ron stood up and grabbed hold of Brenda before dropping the lighter in Robert's blood, sick and petrol soaked crutch, he walked out of the building dragging his wife behind him, the man was laughing at the screams he was walking away from, Brenda was crying at what she had just witnessed and also at what might be waiting for her when they got back home. His wife had put her coat back on but she felt stripped of her feelings, naked and vulnerable to any abuse that might come her way.

CHAPTER 14

Lizzie had just served up an extra-large portion of pleasure to her latest client; the bloke left the room wearing a grin that stretched right across his kisser. The young prostitute had a shower and put on a pair of tracksuit bottoms and a vest; business was at a close for the day and so she joined Claire in the living room.

"I've got some news for you Lizzie, it ain't good I'm afraid."

Lizzie never spoke; she waited for her boss to tell her what she'd found out. Claire lifted up a half-empty glass of red wine and swallowed the remainder in one go. Putting the empty glass on the coffee table the woman licked her lips and sat forward in her chair, "That bloke you wanted back here is brown bread Lizzie, somebody took him and his sidekick out, the pair were messing in bad company and I heard they pissed their boss off and he had 'em taken care of."

Lizzie sat there and let the news sink in; she showed no emotion in either her voice or expression. "That's that fuck out the window I guess, what's on the tele." Inside, the girl was hurting; she now wanted revenge for her brother's death.

Claire was relieved that her nice little earner had taken the news so well; her worries that she might lose the best source of income on her list of employees had now vanished. The boss switched the TV on, and the pair sat back and prepared to enjoy *The Morecambe and Wise Show*.

CHAPTER 15

Ray hadn't had any work for a while and, although he still had a large wedge of cash on him, he was a little bored. On impulse, the henchman decided to return to the scene of his last crime, not something he would normally do, but he figured 'Big H' must still be short of a worker, and he could take him up on the offer of work that he had previously made. Back in the area, Ray sorted some digs, freshened up with a shower and made his way out on to the street. Looking left and right, he spotted a boozer that looked a bit lively; he could hear the music and see bodies going in and out. Ray made his way to the door and walked in. The boozer was close to full, with some people dancing and others just hanging in cliques chatting and laughing. Getting to the bar wasn't easy, but Ray eventually got there, exhaling with relief to celebrate his success before pulling a fiver from his pocket and holding it aloft to get one of the barman's attention. He had to wait several minutes before getting a result, but just as the barman was a ut to pour his drink, he stopped and started to serve another bloke. Ray's eyes widened in disbelief, and his jaw dropped. "Are you for real?" he hollered out, his question was ignored, "Oi! I'm talking to you, where's my fuckin' drink?"

An insignificant little geezer standing next to him tapped him on his arm. "Ron wants a drink mate, he'll be back to you in a minute."

"Who the fuck is Ron?"

"You are better off not knowing, he ain't good news and nobody messes with him."

Ray looked along the bar and saw the ape who had demanded the barman's attention. "He's one big bastard, I'll give him that." Ray then noticed the woman standing next to him, "And handy with his fists if the bird's face is anything to go by."

"If you're happy with your life and your features the way they are, I'd steer well clear mate and keep your comments to yourself."

Mr Insignificant parted with an insipid smile and then moved away. Ray checked the big geezer out again and then gave his bird the once over, tutting at the state of her kisser. He waited for the barman to bring his attention back to him. Ray took his drink, a single malt on the rocks, and handed over the fiver, "Keep the change and thanks for the wait."

The barman smiled a thanks and ignored the remark. With his drink in his hand Ray moved along the bar and pushed himself in next to the blonde with the battered features. "Looks sore lady, did you fall over?" Ray received a nervous look, but no reply; Ray pressed on, "does the big ugly bastard hit men as well or is he just a woman beater?"

Brenda's eyes grew wide as she looked incredulously at the average looking figure asking her these questions; reading the look, Ray guessed he hit blokes too.

"Sorry lady but you look shit scared of the goon, why are you still with him?"

Ron turned his attention towards the upstart with all the gob. "You got something to say mate, then say it to me not the Missus." Ray now had Ron's full attention as Brenda turned away from him and looked at her ol' man.

"Please Ron, no more violence, I can't take anymore."

Brenda started to shake, "Please Ron, no more violence, I can't take anymore." Ron mimicked; he was taking the piss out of his missus; stepping back from the bar he pushed Brenda out of the way and moved closer to Ray.

"Now speak to me, what do you want to know little man."

Ray looked at the man in front of him and lifted his whisky to his lips, swallowing the contents of the glass in one go. He then put his glass on the counter and turned towards Ron, "I was asking the lady if you got off beating on her and if you was brave enough to hit a man too."

"You cheeky little bastard." Ron grabbed at Ray, and the smaller man pulled back out of distance and then moved forward, landing a blow on his attacker's arm. Ron lashed out with a backward swipe, but Ray pulled back again, and it missed; he then moved back in range and smashed a blow in to the big ape's face. The area around the David and Goliath contest had emptied, and the two bouncers were staring at each other, unaware of what they should do; Ron let out a loud growl as he grabbed out at the annoying little bastard in front of him; Ray moved forward and inside the lunge and smashed his head up under the goon's chin, he then brought his knee up and smashed it into Ron's bollocks, the big man yelled out in pain and anger as another right-hander smashed into his face, Ray had popped his set of knuckle dusters on and the big man's face burst open under the impact. Another punch followed, and then another, the claret was flowing freely now, and the big man fell to his knees; a couple of more digs had him horizontal. Ray turned towards Brenda, who was moving towards her ol' man, "leave him and come with me, I'll look after you."

"I can't do that you idiot, you're a dead man walking, and anyway I love him."

Ray looked at the woman, "and he obviously loves you

too; look at the state of your face, for fuck's sake. I'm offering you the chance to have a normal life."

Brenda let out a laugh, "With you? You're no better than him, now go." She turned her attention back to her ol' man; he was still horizontal and covered in claret.

Ray shrugged and made his way out of the boozer; as he walked across the floor everybody moved out of his way, including the two bouncers who couldn't believe what they had just witnessed. Stepping out on to the pavement, he pulled his knuckle dusters off and popped them back in his pocket. Everybody's attention was now focussed on the beaten wreck on the floor.

"I think he needs an ambulance Brenda, shall I call for one." The barman looked genuinely concerned; Brenda was kneeling next to her ol' man crying.

"Yes, yes, please hurry up."

As she spoke, Ron rolled on to his back and lifted his hand up to his face; he felt and then saw the blood, "Where is the little bastard? I'm gonna fuckin' kill him."

The barman cancelled the phone call, several geezers moved forward and went to help Ron get to his feet.

"Fuck off the lot of ya, I don't need your help."

They all stepped back as Ron pulled himself up in to a sitting position; Brenda went to kiss him and received a clump for her troubles. The blow sent her sprawling across the floor, and Ron made an attempt to stand up, but he fell back on the floor. "Bollocks." The big battered bastard rolled over and pulled himself upon his knees; he then attempted standing up again and staggered forward, sending several people sprawling across the floor. Brenda had just taken what she hoped was her final blow from Ron as she walked out of the pub and clocked Ray, who was a couple of hundred yards up the road, she called out after him, and he turned around and walked back to her, neither spoke as she grabbed his arm and they walked off together.

Ray had just broken Rule No.1 by involving himself with a female, but even worse, a married one. "Nothing good's gonna come out of this," he told himself, "but what the fuck, let's not worry about the now and just enjoy the moment, a little bit of fun can't do any harm to either of us."

CHAPTER 16

Lizzie needed to chat with Claire and persuade her boss to cut her a bit of slack. The girl needed to find out who had popped her brother John, the bastard had dished out a fair bit of misery in his little sister's direction, but she was still pissed off that somebody had taken him out, so Lizzie needed the name of the boozer where Claire had met Alan.

"Fuck, life can be so complicated at times." Lizzie sighed and prepared for her next customer; after he left, it was the end of another successful day for her and Claire, successful because Lizzie enjoyed her work when she had full sex with a customer, she orgasmed and whooped with pleasure during the session, and if it was a hand or blow job she felt excitement at the moment just before her client climaxed. The men were weak and vulnerable then and just after, and Lizzie felt all-powerful. It was, for her, exhilarating, which was probably the reason why she was so good at her job.

The little prossie showered and then popped on a tracksuit bottom and tee-shirt before joining her boss in the living room. As Lizzie entered the room, Claire laughed, "You're one noisy little fucker when you're on the job young lady, I don't think I've ever had a girl like you work for me before. Most of 'em are working to feed a habit, you though, well, you seem to love your work."

Lizzie blushed at her boss's statement before laughing too. "I do, I really do."

Plonking herself down on the sofa, Lizzie continued, "Claire what was the name of the boozer where you met the bloke with the big cock?"

The question took Lizzie's boss by surprise, and she blurted out the name of the pub before asking why her employee wanted to know.

"Fuck, I've just dropped a bollock there," Claire thought. "Why the need to know Lizzie?" The employee's face was expressionless as she gave her reply, "Oh! No real reason, just wondered where you met the blokes you bring back to me, that's all."

Claire frowned, "Not thinking of going it alone are you Lizzie?"

The question carried a threatening tone that unsettled the girl.

"Blimey No Claire, I'd never do that; I love living here and working for you. You're like the mum I never had.

Claire smiled, "You better not be lying to me you little fucker." Claire's thoughts were read by Lizzie, and she gave her boss a reassuring smile before changing the subject.

"Shall we watch a bit of telly before we eat?"

The pair settled back on their seats and focussed their attention in the direction of the picture box; neither of them were 100% at ease.

After a while, Claire got up out of her chair and walked to the phone that sat atop a table in the hallway. She made two phone calls, the first one was to the local Indian restaurant, she ordered two ruby's, two naans and one rice. When she made the second call, her voice dropped almost to a whisper, and when she put the receiver down to end the call, the woman felt more relaxed. It was a positive Claire that returned to Lizzie. "I've ordered dinner, it will be here in ten minutes, I'll pour us both a drink Lizzie and we can toast the future."

Claire poured a generous amount of vodka on to some ice and then added just a splash of orange juice; she gave one to Lizzie and then held her glass up, "Here's to a long and happy future Lizzie, a shit free one too."

Lizzie lifted her glass in Claire's direction before taking a mouthful and swallowing it down. The strength of the drink took her by surprise and made her splutter, causing Claire to laugh. The mood lightened a little, but Lizzie's boss had delivered her message. When the Ruby Murrays arrived, they were eaten in near silence; both women's heads were full of thoughts. Lizzie wondering about her brother's killer, Claire wondering whether the second phone call had been necessary. "Better safe than sorry!" she told herself.

CHAPTER 17

Ray took Brenda to a quiet little boozer a few blocks away from the one they had just walked out of. He bought two drinks, and the pair sat in a secluded little corner away from the other drinkers, they were all couples, but Ray guessed that he and Brenda were the only two in there that had known each other for no longer than a few minutes.

"I don't know what I'm doing here really! What's your name anyway?" Brenda looked nervously around and got up to leave. Ray grabbed her hand and looked at her.

"It's Ray and please don't go, sit down and enjoy your drink, let's have a little chat, maybe another drink before we decide what to do, anyway I think you going back to your ol' man right now would be a big mistake, he'd probably rearrange your features again and you don't need that."

Ray kept hold of the woman's hand, "Please sit down, like I said, let's have a drink before we decide what we're gonna do next."

Brenda sat back down and released an enormous sigh, "I guess you're right Ray, but I'm gonna have to go back sometime and cop that beating I deserve." The combination of stress and fear got the better of the woman and she started to cry; Ray took out a clean folded hankie and passed it to her.

"You don't deserve being hit by that big ugly bastard,

and I've just proved he ain't so tough, why did he hit you anyway?"

Brenda used Ray's hankie to wipe her eyes and then told her saviour all about Robert and what her ol' man had done to him. "He's gonna be after you next Ray and if I was you I'd be having it away from here, go back to where you came from and put a bit of distance between the pair of you. Better still, move abroad."

Ray laughed. "He should be the worried man really darling, what if I go back and give him another good hiding, anyway what's your name?"

"Brenda."

"Okay, Brenda, let's enjoy this drink and some time together and forget your ol' man for now.

Ray lifted his glass off the table and proffered it in Brenda's direction; the woman sighed for a second time before forcing a smile on to her bruised face and lifting her glass too. They clinked glasses mid-air and then drank."

"You're gorgeous when you smile, Brenda, and I have to say you've got a cracking little figure, you seem far too nice to be with that big ugly bastard if you don't mind me saying, anyway do you fancy another drink?"

Ray finished his whisky and stood up; Brenda finished her drink too and passed her glass to him, parting with another smile as she did so.

When they had finished their second drink, they left the boozer holding hands. Having been away from Ron and receiving some much-needed attention, Brenda was feeling pretty pleased with herself and had told Ray she was happy to spend the night with him. Once outside, Ray hailed a passing taxi and the pair set off for a hotel in the next borough; putting some more distance between them and Ron made Brenda feel more at ease.

The sex with Ray had been great, but Brenda had wanted it to be more than that; she had wanted to be making love with her big ape. She now felt as guilty as fuck with what she had done, but instead of jumping up and out of bed the little blonde, not really knowing why, chose to snuggle up to Ray and the closeness she felt helped ease the guilt a little. Brenda felt relaxed and surrounded by a strange kind of happiness in Ray's company, so she decided to stay the night with him, he was good in the sack anyway, and it had been a long time since she'd had sex. Deciding her happiness could only survive a short time before they were destroyed by a return to normality and Ron, she would have to wake up before Ray then sneak out the room and have it on her toes, probably go to her sister's place and beg her to say she'd spent the night there. Her sister Shirley loved her and hated Ron, but she also lived in fear of the big ugly bastard. Brenda knew that she'd lie for her, but she also knew that her sister wouldn't be happy doing it in case Ron found out the truth. So, plan sorted, Brenda relaxed and grabbed hold of Ray's cock; she wanted more sex, and Ray was happy to oblige.

When the fuck was over they laid back on the bed and Ray closed his eyes, wondering what tomorrow would bring. One half of him hoped that Brenda would still be there with him; maybe he'd found his happy ever after bird. The other half told him to get a grip, "wake up and smell the coffee you mug", he told himself. How could it be happy ever after with somebody else's missus, especially when that somebody else was Ron? The bloke had connections and would probably be able to track him down easy enough. "He'd kill me for sure," Ray told himself, "probably shoot me cos he wouldn't want to risk a second beating."

Ray opened his eyes and turned to face Brenda. "God she's beautiful," he told himself, "and just look at that figure." A standing prick has no conscience, so they say, and that's what Ray was in possession of once again.

Laying with Brenda after the sex, Ray needed to think again about tomorrow. "Better have it on me toes before she wakes up and put some distance between us, maybe I'll have to go abroad for a while just like she had suggested". As good as the fucks were and as beautiful as the bird was, too, Ray didn't want it to be his last one. "What have you done you mug?"

Ray knew he'd fucked up big time, and Brenda, who chose to snuggle up against Ray again, was having the same thoughts. The pair feigned sleep and waited for the opportunity to have it on their toes. Each of them had a plan, but neither of them were confident that it would work. Brenda shuddered at the thought of the good hiding she'd be getting, and Ray feared for his life. Then it hit him, "hold on you mug," he thought, "the answer's easy, take Ron out first and then nick his missus, win-win."

The thought of popping the big ugly bastard excited Ray, and he opened his eyes and looked at Brenda; he took her hand and put it on his erection; she opened her eyes and laughed, "fucking hell Ray, not again." Brenda rolled on to her back and welcomed her stud in, releasing a loud moan as he entered her.

"Heaven here I come," she exclaimed.

After the sex, Ray held Brenda in his arms and kissed her forehead; he suddenly decided that he wasn't going anywhere in the morning and hoped his newfound bit of happiness wasn't either. However, although Brenda was happy and felt safe in Ray's arms, she continued to tell herself that it couldn't last." I belong to Ron unfortunately and at some point I've gotta go back and face the music." She cuddled into Ray and hoped he would soon nod off. Unfortunately for her, the plan went tits up when she fell asleep first. It had been ages since Brenda had been filled with such bliss and the contentment she felt had overcome her anxiety. Ray listened to her gentle breathing as she slept and stuck a kiss on her forehead, but the vision of Ron's head exploding when he pulled the trigger on the gun now filled his thoughts; he could see the bullet entering and exiting the big ape's head, and he would not be joining Brenda in the land of nod even though he wanted to, Ray was way too high for that to happen.

CHAPTER 18

Lizzie entered the boozer feeling a bit nervous, the butterflies were doing the business in her stomach and she very nearly turned around and had it on her toes. "Take a deep breath and get a grip!" Heeding her own advice, she inhaled and pushed the door open. The young girl was nicely turned out and you would never have guessed her profession from looking at her. She wasn't the prettiest of girls (I might have mentioned that before!), but she had a tidy little figure and her entrance turned a few heads with several geezers throwing out positive vibes; Lizzie felt a bit more at ease and made her way to the bar where she ordered a vodka and orange. She never noticed the bloke that had been on her tail since she left home and now stood a couple of feet away from her; he ordered tonic water; the barman gave him a bit of a look but then poured his drink.

Lizzie took a sip of her drink and then looked around at the people in the bar. "My brother's murderer could be in here right now," the thought gave Lizzie the willies, and she visibly shuddered, "but how would I know who it was and who do I go to first to get some info? Fuck this ain't gonna be easy!"

Lizzie resigned herself to the fact that she didn't really have a Scooby about what to do next. She took another swig of her vodka and orange, she didn't even know what to say if she did know who to ask, "Hello, did you kill my brother and the nasty little bastard that knocked around with him?" Thinking that was a bit too direct, Lizzie finished her drink and left the boozer. "Need to come up with some sort of a plan before I come back here again."

The anonymous bloke left his tonic water and followed Lizzie out of the bar and on to the street; he then followed her home.

"What a waste of a night." The bloke walked past Lizzie's address and made his way home; he would phone the madam in the morning and tell her what had happened.

Claire didn't know whether to feel relieved or remain apprehensive when she received the news.

"Okay thanks," she sighed, "I'll call back if I need any more favours." She hung up the phone and walked into the kitchen where she found Lizzie tucking into a slice of toast and cup of tea.

"Morning Lizzie, anything exciting happen last night?" Claire stuck a smile on the end of the question as Lizzie looked up and mumbled her reply because her mouth was full of toast.

"No, I had one drink and came home, do you wanna cup of tea?"

"Yeah okay!"

While she poured her boss the cuppa, Lizzie had a thought, why not come clean about the two blokes that were dead and why she needed to find the bastard that had carried out the killings.

"Maybe later, I've got a few fucks lined up for today and I don't wanna do anything to spoil my fun."

Claire looked at her little gold mine and could see the cogs turning inside the girl's head. "There's something going on with you young lady and I need to find out what that something is."

The day passed with Lizzie and her customers all having

fun; every fuck had resulted in an orgasm for both the customer and Lizzie and had been accompanied by loud sighs of satisfaction. Lizzie had teased every erection and played it to the max before making it come. When the explosion occurred, every customer spent a little time in sex heaven before floating back to earth, and Claire counted the pounds as they rolled in.

"That girl has something, and it makes me money like you wouldn't Adam and Eve' it; I can't afford to lose her." Claire needed to know what the attraction to this one bloke was; she didn't believe it was the size of his cock, and anyway with the geezer 'brown bread' surely that was the end of the matter, "I'm gonna ask her outright what the fuck is going on and if I don't get the answer I want, not want really, more like deserve, I'll have to think of a way to get her to spill the beans, which might prove a bit painful for her.

Lizzie wasn't the only prostitute working for Claire but as the top earner and being the only one that genuinely enjoyed her job; she was the only one that Claire let share her living room; the other girls had their own room with their own TV in it. It was fair to say that the relationship between boss and worker with these two was unique, and Claire wanted to keep it that way. The two women were sat on the sofa with a glass of wine in their hands; both took a large mouthful of their drink and sighed almost at the same time, "okay, here goes", the thought was simultaneous as were their first words "Listen, I've got something to..." The pair laughed, it was an awkward noise that escaped their lips, and both stopped talking for a second. "Carry on!" the two words were in unison again, and another awkward laugh followed, and a pregnant pause came after that. Eventually, after what seemed like forever to both of them, Claire broke the silence,

"What's the connection between you and the bloke that

got popped the other night Lizzie, and don't give me that same shit about the size of his cock cos I think that's a load of bollocks young lady."

"Blimey, where'd that come from and why is she worried about him?"

"Well, are you gonna come clean young lady?"

Lizzie looked at her boss and then took another mouthful of wine before going full pelt with her confession. When she had finished, Claire was sitting there open-mouthed.

"I hope there's no flies in here," Lizzie laughed after her comment; the laugh was a nervous one. Was her boss gonna help her, or was she pissed off big time? The answer wasn't forthcoming as Claire stood up and walked to the sideboard where she filled her glass with more wine; she then walked over to Lizzie with the bottle in her hand and did the same for her.

"Come on, say something and put me out of my misery." Claire did not reply, and Lizzie thought that she should have kept her gob shut. "I've fucked things up now, bollocks!"

Several minutes passed before Claire answered; her expression said she was undecided as to how to react to her employee's confession.

""I'm tired, Lizzie and going to bed now; maybe we'll talk some more tomorrow, maybe."

Claire left the room and a confused girl behind.

"Tomorrow, maybe!" What the fuck does that mean?"

Lizzie wouldn't be getting much kip tonight.

Just as she had thought Lizzie spent the night tossing and turning, and for most of the time there was no shut-eye. She came down to breakfast looking tired and feeling irritable, Claire's look wasn't too far away from being the same as hers. They sat opposite each other, both cradling a cup of tea in their hands and neither talking. When she'd finished her tea Lizzie made to leave the room; as she reached the door she turned around and looked at Claire.

"I'm going back to bed Claire, don't feel great so need the day off, get one of the other girls to cover for me." Lizzie turned and went to walk out.

"Whoa" Stop right there, young lady. You ain't having a day off, these customers want you, and they'll have you."

"But, I…"

"No buts Lizzie, go and get yourself ready and after you've satisfied your last customer we can talk, I may be able to help you find the bloke that killed your brother, what we do then fuck knows."

CHAPTER 19

"Listen Brenda, I need to pop out for a bit, d'you wanna wait here for me? I won't be long."

Ray had been up and showered before dressing in yesterday's clobber. When he came back into the bedroom, Brenda was sitting up in bed wearing a pasted-on smile that told Ray she was shit scared.

"I'll book this room on my way out and have breakfast brought up to you."

"I dunno Ray, I should probably get back to Ron and face the music, I'll get my sis to say I spent the night there."

Ray moved over to the bed and sat next to Brenda; he took hold of her hand and placed a delicate kiss on her forehead.

"Listen Brenda, I know you're scared of that big ugly bastard you married but you don't have to be. See me, well I can take care of him and then you and me can be together, happy ever after and all that stuff, what d'ya say?"

A nervous laugh fell out, "Oh! Ray, happy ever after aint ever gonna happen, Ron won't let it, I'm his property and he won't just let me go."

The woman sat up and cupped Ray's boat in her hands, kissing him softly on the lips. "Best do things my way, better all round I think. I'll probably cop another good hiding but I guess it's what I deserve anyway."

Ray kissed her back but with a bit more passion, and

Brenda started crying.

"No need for tears girl, I've got this one covered, I can make happiness happen for you."

His eyes were begging Brenda to agree with his way, but her's were telling him otherwise.

"I can't let you pop him Ray, if that's what you're saying, I guess I love the big ugly bastard in a warped sort of way and I'm sure he loves me too. I'll get dressed and head off home," there was a pause while Brenda looked into Ray's eyes and sighed, "it's for the best."

"You're the first bird I've ever had these sort of feelings for Brenda, I'm putting my life on the line here to be with you but it's what I want and I think it's what you want too."

Brenda laughed. "I'll get dressed Ray and be on my way." She got out of the bed, collected her clothes and made her way to the bathroom. Ray was one unhappy bunny,

" what the fuck! I really don't understand."

On the doorstep of the hotel, just five minutes later, Brenda went up on tiptoes and stuck a smacker on Ray's lips; she then pressed her forefinger against them and said goodbye before turning and walking away.

"Bollocks!" Ray waited a while before deciding to follow her, "I ain't letting her go that easy."

His pursuit of the woman that he had fallen head over heels for had started off half-heartedly, "do I need this hassle?" he asked himself. He then told himself that his career would also be over, and as a result, all of his speed left him, and he went to turn around and walk away.

"Bollocks, I can't leave her to face another good hiding from that mug she married." His speed increased until he was almost running, it didn't take him long to catch up with Brenda, and he shouted out for her to stop when he was ten yards away. Brenda obeyed and turned to face Ray. A big happy grin appeared on her boat, and she opened her arms to allow Ray to walk into an embrace.

"I thought you weren't gonna follow and I would have to go back to the ol' man and cop that good hiding."

Ray held on to the woman. "If you want to be with me, why did you walk away?"

The poor man was confused, "Will a man ever understand a woman?" He was sure the answer to that question was a big fat 'NO'.

"I needed to know that you meant what you said and that I wasn't somebody you just wanted to fuck."

"That's all I wanted it to be." He told himself.

"It was never just that Brenda" was what fell out of his mouth, "fuckin liar" was the next thought that he had. He couldn't understand or explain what had happened and why he'd fallen head over heels in love with her, but the bottom line was that he had. "Next move mug" was the next three words that entered his bonce.

"Let's get away from here first girl, still a bit too close to the big ape for comfort."

Brenda laughed. "Have you got a horse parked up somewhere my knight in shining armour?"

"No, but I've got a car parked a few blocks away."

Brenda copped hold of Ray's arm, and they did a 180-degree turn and walked off as a couple. Their stroll was accompanied by a bit of a stutter due to their thoughts and emotions being a bit muddled. Both were asking themselves the same question. "Am I doing the right thing or have I just lost the plot?"

Neither of them could answer that question.

Welded together by a sex manufactured sweat and sharing a need for love and life, the pair lay side by side in another hotel bed. They had taken part in several emotionally charged fucks, but once they were over, reality jumped back out again and slapped them both in their kissers.

"The future, what if there wasn't one and nothing happened past these next few sexually charged days." For Brenda, it was comforting and warmly reassuring to feel loved again, but the image of Ron's big scary boat kept leaping out at her and scaring the poor woman to fuck. "What happens if he catches up with us, I'm dead, that's what."

Brenda pulled herself closer to Ray and prayed that he would be able to protect her. Her heart wanted the answer to be yes, her head said 'No'.

Ray was certain that he could add Ron's scalp to his list of hits. It would be the first one that he hadn't been paid for, but he felt it would be the most rewarding. His paid work had him take out unknowns; it made his life easier. Popping someone, or even just inflicting a life-changing amount of pain on them gave Ray a buzz, and he had proved to be good at his job. Stripping Ron of his future and relieving a lot of misery from several people's lives, most importantly, his and Brenda's would, he hoped, give him the same buzz.

What would life hold for him after that? He didn't have a 'scooby doo.'

"Let's get rid of the big ape first and see if we can then move forward with this relationship."

Showered and dressed, the pair headed north, where they would hideaway for a couple of days and make plans for the immediate future; neither of them could look much further ahead than that anyway. Removing the big ape was their first priority, and if that went 'tits up', there wouldn't be a future to worry about.

Stopping at a High Street, the pair did some clothes shopping. Ray, because of the state of Brenda's boat' copped a few questioning looks from both passers-by and staff, but he wouldn't be returning to this neck of the woods any time soon, so did he give a fuck what people thought? The answer was another big fat, "No".

They had lunch together before making their way to the East Coast. "Might as well have a little holiday together Brenda while we make our plans for the future." Ray had a bounce in his step that told Brenda he was certain things would work outright, but her bounce was not on show; Ron's face, full of anger and roaring abuse, was still haunting her along with the vision of Robert being set alight after their brief encounter.

CHAPTER 20

Once again, Lizzie and Claire were perched on their armchairs and holding a glass of wine in their hands; Lizzie waited for her boss to start the conversation, Claire seemed to be enjoying her tipple and in no rush to start talking, so for Lizzie time seemed to have stopped, this Claire imposed pause in her life was proving to be painful, almost everlasting, when her boss suddenly started to speak. Lizzie let out a big sigh at the sudden outburst of noise and hoped she would like what she was about to hear.

"I have connections Lizzie, people in the know and I could probably find out why your brother and his partner came to such an untimely and sticky end, but…"

"There's always a but, here comes the bit I ain't gonna like."

The next few sentences proved Lizzie's thoughts to be right.

"Your brother was no saint, he was mixed up with the wrong people young lady and so an untimely death ain't so surprising. It wasn't an accident, it was a professional hit and finding out who did it wouldn't be too difficult but with the easy bit out of the way the hard bit would be trying to exact some sort of revenge. You start messing with the type of people your brother was mixed up with and it could and most possibly would go pear shaped for you and you might even be meeting up with your brother much sooner than you wanted to."

Lizzie looked at her boss and believed she was talking sense but fuck that, the young lady, as Claire had just called her, wanted revenge for John's death.

"He was my brother Claire; I can't just let it go, sorry."

It was the response Claire had expected, so there was no look of surprise on her 'boat'; the woman was wearing a concerned one instead.

"I've put a few feelers out and word will get back to me soon but once I have a name or names for you that's me done, I like life and ain't ready to meet my maker just yet, besides I don't think there's a place for me up there, I'm probably going to hell and I ain't in any kind of rush to meet that horny little bastard."

Lizzie laughed, "Horned, not horny!"

"I don't give a fuck what he is, I ain't ready to meet him."

The mood had lightened, and they both laughed, but it darkened again with great speed as Lizzie declared her intentions; she was going to kill the man responsible. "An eye for an eye Claire, nothing less." The tele was turned on and the rest of the evening spent in silence. While Lizzie's thoughts were of revenge for her brother's untimely exit, Claire's thoughts were about how much money she would lose after Lizzie had taken her last breath.

The next few days saw Lizzie continue to please both her customers and herself and the profit continued to pour in for a happy Claire; it was smiles all round until the boss lady received a note containing the name of John and Alan's killer. She looked at the name for an age. "I don't know this geezer and I need a few more days money before I say anything to the best little prossie I've ever employed." Claire stuffed the note in a drawer.

Lizzie remained patient for a couple of weeks; she

carried on causing men's cocks to explode into happy orgasms and accompanying them with her own, while Claire's till continued to ring happy'.

"Still no news Claire, it's been a couple of weeks since our last chat."

Claire looked at Lizzie and saw the need to know, staring out at her from the girl's eyes.

"Seems the bloke wasn't a local and that's making it harder to come up with anything. "The guilt that Claire was feeling caused her to look away, and Lizzie picked up on the negativity.

"You being straight with me Claire?"

"Of course Lizzie, listen I'll push a bit harder for you, okay?"

Lizzie sighed heavily, and Claire was happy that her bluff had worked, but the uneasy silence that had occupied most of their time together over the last couple of weeks remained.

"I don't think she's being straight with me, the bitch." Lizzie was not happy.

"I guess I'll have to tell her soon and to be honest what's she gonna do? Can't see how she's gonna track this bloke down anyway."

Claire let another couple of days pass before she handed the piece of paper with Ray's name on it to Lizzie.

"Be careful where you go with this information Lizzie, we don't want it going tits up for you, these are dangerous people you're gonna be mixing with."

With a sudden pang of guilt grabbing her, Claire also told Lizzie that a man known as 'Big H' ordered the hit and that her brother and his sidekick were working for him at the time.

Lizzie felt a bit easier with the knowledge she had gained and thanked her boss. She decided to do nothing for a couple of days except mull things over in her mind. If this

'Big H' geezer had ordered the hit on Alan and John while they were working for him, she guessed he must have been pretty pissed with what they'd done. Lizzie needed to know what line of business 'Big H' was involved with; maybe she needed to go back to the boozer she had visited before and see if she could find anyone willing to help her with her enquiries.

CHAPTER 21

Ray left Brenda in the chalet they had rented for a couple of weeks; she knew where he was going and just hoped everything went to plan.

"I've got an address and this," he waved his piece at Brenda "so I don't even have to get close to the bastard."

Five hours later, Ray was sitting outside Ron's house looking for signs of activity from within. "Back to the waiting game I guess," he told himself and settled himself back in his seat.

Ron stood at the bar in the boozer and ordered himself a beer; he didn't see the slip of a girl squeeze in beside him but turned and looked when he felt a tap on his arm.

"You could buy me a drink if you wanted to." The girl smiled up at him,

"And why would I wanna do that?"

Lizzie stuck her hand on his crutch and gave his cock a squeeze.

"I'll make it worth your while," Lizzie lifted her eyebrows and licked her top lip while massaging Ron's handful of manhood. The laugh that exited Ron's lips was deep and almost scary, but Lizzie didn't let go.

"And get this cheeky little bitch whatever she wants as well."

The massage continued, and Ron let out a moan.

"Okay lady, we'll drink up and take this back to my place."

"I hope to fuck you can tell me what I need to know you big ugly bastard" is what went through Lizzie's mind – "Sounds good to me" is what came out of her mouth.

Ron was taken aback by this young girl and wondered why she had approached him, but it had been a long time since he'd shagged anyone, and he could fuck this bird and then throw her out. She wasn't a patch on Brenda to look at, but she'd excited the big ape, and now he needed to unload.

When the car pulled on to the drive Ray's face lit up. "Here we go, time to remove the ugly bastard from mine and Brenda's lives," Ray removed the pistol from inside his jacket and fitted the silencer before getting out of his motor and walking across the road. Lizzie gave Ron's crutch another squeeze; this action told her she'd kept his interest. The pair got out of Ron's motor, closed the doors and made their way to the front door.

"Bollocks, who's that with him?"

Ray was not happy to find Brenda's ol' man with another bird; it wasn't jealousy, just the fact that he'd have to pop both of them. He took aim and fired; the bullet left the gun and then entered the back of Ron's head; a split second later, it flew out of the front and buried itself in the front wall of the recipient's house. Ron fell forward, poleaxed, the bastard hit his concrete drive, and blood ran freely from the newly made hole he had just acquired. Lizzie screamed and turned to face Ray; fear was written across her face in big, bold capital letters as she clocked the view of the killer. Ray had the pistol directed on her, and he squeezed the trigger. Lizzie screamed again, but the noise was cut short as the bullet hit its target, the girl fell forward, and Ray turned away; he took off the silencer and then replaced the pistol in his jacket pocket and strode confidently towards his set of wheels. "Mission accomplished." Ray allowed himself a satisfied smile, "Now back to Brenda and the rest of the holiday."

When Lizzie's scared look had made contact with the cold and confident stare of her killer, the fear she felt had frozen her to the spot, but then the need to survive kicked in, and the prossie moved her head, the bullet had only grazed the side of her nut, but she collapsed to the floor anyway. The stinging sensation the bullet had caused her was painful, but Lizzie bit down on her lip and stopped the squeal escaping from her lips; alive but in pain, Lizzie lay motionless for an age after the car, driven by Ron's murderer, had pulled away. Ray's ice-cold look was staring out at her from inside her brain; it was a look and a face that weren't going away any time soon.

Ray switched the car radio on and listened to the music; he drove to a B and B and booked in for the night. The next morning he would get up early and make the return journey to the East Coast, and he hoped to a woman who would be happy with what he had just accomplished.

When she finally raised the courage to move, Lizzie got herself into an upright position, the warmth from the blood running down the side of her face confirmed the fact that she had been hit, but she knew that she was lucky to still be alive and as she looked at the corpse only a few yards from her Lizzie burst into tears. The whole terrifying episode had caused her to piss herself.

The girl couldn't drive a car, so that meant she wouldn't be 'half inching' Ron's motor and driving back to Claire. The damage to her 'boat' and the pissy pants meant she couldn't hail a cab or jump on a bus, but it was time to leave the scene of this particular crime behind. 'Shanks's Pony' it would have to be; Lizzie stuck her head back in the goon's car and found a scarf in the glove compartment; she tied it around her nut and covered the wound before setting off. Her exit was only moments before a neighbour came out and saw Ron lying in a pool of claret and rang the Old Bill.

Lizzie finally got back to Claire, who gave her little cash

maker a big hug after she had sighed with relief at the girl's survival. "You're gonna have a nasty 'mars bar' down the side of your 'boat race' girl.

The pair of them began to laugh; neither knew why. It was a mixture of fear and relief; Lizzie was relieved that she was still alive and Claire still had her best worker. They both shared a fear for the future.

Claire called her own doctor to the house; she didn't need the questions that would accompany a visit to the hospital. The doctor, who received a decent 'wedge' for his troubles, applied the stitches needed to close up the channel left by the bullet; he asked no questions and left with just the one comment "It'll leave a scar."

"You better have a couple of days off Lizzie, but stick around here, I think that makes sense."

"If I'm staying here I may as well work," and that is what the prossie did. It was smiles all round, the boss, the worker and her clients were all very happy!

The 'Old Bill' arrived at the scene and called in the murder, they went through the motions, but no great effort would be made on their part to find the killer of a known gangster. It was one less for them to worry about, their only concern was that this one killing could have repercussions, and a spate of murders could follow. "Let's hope this is a one off, too much bloody paperwork to be done if it ain't." The DCI in charge of the case stuck his hands in his coat pocket and took out a packet of cigarettes and a lighter; he lit one up and inhaled deeply before blowing the smoke out and making his way back to his motor.

The lack of interest shown by the 'Old Bill' was more than made up for by the need to identify the 'shooter' from all the local villains. Would any of their lives be at risk? Ron's killer needed to be found, and 'sorted'. It also came to light that no one had seen Brenda since the night of the beating. Was she involved, or had she also been bumped off, and was it the same bloke that they had seen administer that beating to Ron in his local that had pulled the trigger? The community of local villains were feeling uncomfortable with Ron's death and the disappearance of his missus, and so a couple of them decided that it was time to give 'Big H' a visit and get some answers. Ron's boss, Robert, wanted answers too; he'd just lost his right-hand man and didn't know why but was worried that he could be next on the list. He had witnessed Ron's good hiding in the boozer and was eager to have the culprit found. Fagin, as he was known to by most of the locals, put a handsome price on the head of the offender and then sat back and waited. Brenda's disappearance was of no consequence to him, so when his missus asked him to find her, the promise that he made to her was an empty one.

CHAPTER 22

"She was in the wrong place at the wrong time Claire, ain't nothing else gonna happen." Claire let out a sigh of relief and made to leave 'Big H's' office. "By the way I think the bloke holding the gun was the same one that took her brother out."

'Big H' winked at Claire, "the bastard knows it was the same bloke cos he probably employed him to take Ron out, but why?"

Would Claire share that information with Lizzie? She didn't think she would. "What she doesn't know can't hurt her."

"Ron's boss has stuck a price tag on the geezer's head", Harry continued, so she'll get her justice anyway, just a question of time."

That statement made it something that Claire would now share with Lizzie.

The young girl wasn't sure that she was capable of murder as angry as she was over the death of her brother, so when Claire announced that Ray had a price on his head at the breakfast table the next day, she received the news from her boss with a sense of relief. "I can get on with my job now Claire, thanks for the info and everything."

Claire hugged her employee, Lizzie hugged her back and, as her boss stepped back, Lizzie went up on her toes and planted a kiss on Claire's lips. The pair looked at each other, and with no words from either, a message was sent and received. Claire cupped Lizzie's face in her hand and kissed her back, Lizzie grabbed a handful of her boss's arse, and Claire returned the favour; the kisses continued until Claire took hold of the girl's hand and led her to the bedroom where they undressed each other before falling on to the bed. The passion and desire for each other continued all the way to an orgasm.

Afterwards, Lizzie's thoughts were, "Wow! What just happened, I didn't think I'd like it that much."

Claire's were the exact opposite. "How the fuck did I let that happen, where does the relationship go from here?"

The pair showered separately, and Lizzie got ready for her first customer; Claire stayed in her room. That evening after dinner, Claire spoke first. "That was a one off young lady, I don't know why it happened but it won't happen again. Things go back to how they were, okay!" Claire knew the statement was the right one but did she believe it? She wasn't sure.

The revelation hurt Lizzie, "I hope you don't mean that," she thought. "Okay, that's fine by me", came out, and the girl turned away and switched the tele on.

Ray made the journey back to the east coast, unaware of the bounty that had just been placed on his head. Brenda greeted Ray with a smile and a big sigh of relief. "You're back and safe."

"And Ron's no more." Ray smiled at the little blonde and held his arms out to her; Brenda obliged and walked into his embrace; one part of her was happy with the news, but another part held a tiny bit of regret, their marriage hadn't been all bad, and she had loved Ron, but those feelings had just been taken from her by somebody else, and she wasn't sure how she felt about that. "By the way Brenda Ron had company with him, a woman and they seemed pretty tight, unfortunately I had to take her out as well."

"What a bastard, good riddance to the big bully", the revelation had angered Brenda but only momentarily as she turned her attention back to the man in front of her, " Do you think we have a future Ray and do you think we are safe now or will Ron's boss cop the hump and want revenge, is he gonna come after the two of us or pay some of his employees to take us out?" Brenda was wearing a look of despair as Ray took half a pace back and cupped her face in his hands, "Let's go celebrate, what d'ya say, a couple of beers and a bit of grub."

The assassin had dismissed Brenda's questions and followed up his words with a kiss on her forehead and then her lips. "Let's get out of here." He took hold of her hand and led his first-ever real love interest out of the apartment, where they were greeted by sunshine and a blue sky. "And after we've eaten we can take a walk on the beach." Ray was still on a high after his double shooting, there was no room in his head for any negative thoughts, and as Brenda took hold of his arm and they set off together, he felt light and content.

"Fuck the future," Claire thought. "I should be enjoying the now."

Big H, for a price, gave Robert, Ron's boss, Ray's phone number. "Shame you're taking him out Robert, he's good at what he does."

Robert walked out of Big H's office without a reply and left him to count the wedge he'd just handed over.

Ray and Brenda were walking along the beach when Ray's phone rang. It was his second phone, so he knew it was a work-related call.

"Hey 'Big H' what is it?"

"This ain't Big H you little fuck, he's just gone and sold you down the river. Enjoy the next few days arsehole, they're gonna be your last."

The phone went dead and the colour drained from Ray's face.

"Who was that Ray?" Brenda looked concerned.

"Nobody, nothing to worry about." Ray returned the phone to his pocket and smiled, "this is the life Brenda and the start of our future together." He gave Brenda a kiss, "let's take our shoes off and go for a paddle." Ray plonked his arse on the beach and pulled Brenda down with him; she giggled.

"You're nuts Ray, but why not."

Moments later, the pair, hand in hand, were running towards the sea.

"The little fat bastard has sold me out." His bubble of happiness had been punctured by the phone call, and Ray's feet had landed back on the ground. However, his new love interest was armed with both a repair kit and pump and with the damage repaired, Ray's feelings were lifted once more, "Oh! That's fuckin' cold." Brenda shrieked as the water grabbed at her ankles; Ray laughed and lifted her into his arms, Brenda cradled his neck with her arms, and they kissed again, Ray started to walk and then run, Brenda was shrieking with laughter, "Put me down you nutter, put me down before we go arse over…"

Ray lost his footing, and the pair fell forward before Brenda could say "tit".

They laughed together and then started kissing, Ray looked around and saw that the beach was empty, and he had a hard-on; he removed Brenda's knickers and then got his cock out.

"You're fuckin' mad Ray, you really are." As he entered her, the little blonde let out a moan of delight and then laughed.

"I'm fuckin' mad too," she shouted; it was Ray's turn to laugh. They were both oblivious to the cold water that kept grabbing at them and then falling away.

Robert's contract was raising a lot of interest amongst the 'lower echelons' of society; they all wanted the money and thought "How hard can it be to pull the trigger of a gun." Several had already popped somebody, so it didn't bother them but finding Ray would be the hard bit, especially for those who didn't even know what he looked like.

"I need a photo of the corpse before I hand over the cash."

Raymond Connor was very much a wanted man now, and Lizzie took to doing a bit of thinking. "I know what this bloke looks like, so that gives me a head start. The face of the killer plagued her thoughts most of her non-working hours. Did she have it in her to take someone out? "For that sort of money, I think I could," she told herself.

So the list of wannabe killers was now plus one, and Lizzie considered herself to be a serious contender.

A couple of weeks passed, with Ray and Brenda continuing their relationship very much besotted with each other. Brenda hadn't received so much attention in a long time, and every day when Ray told her that he loved her, she found herself elevated to that special place, 'Cloud No.9'.

Ray loved the distraction caused by his new love's presence, but that phone call hung over him like a dark cloud, a cloud he needed to burst. As they lay together, Ray asked a question that put Brenda on edge.

"Do you have a passport?"

Why did it upset her, she wasn't sure, but a move abroad didn't sound like a good option to her, "Yes, but it's in the house."

"Then let's go get it, I think we need some time away so things can settle here."

Brenda sat up in the bed, wearing a concerned look, "We don't know who will be at the house, Robert may well have someone there waiting patiently to take either of us out, or better still both of us."

Ray laughed at Brenda's comment. "Nobody knows you're with me so why would they be at your place?"

Ray wasn't sure that they wouldn't be there, though. "Somebody has to be missing her, and if they've put two and two together and made four, then she could have a point.

"Listen, I'll go in to the house and get it, you can wait in the car for me. Where d'ya fancy going, France or Spain?"

Brenda lay back in bed and faced Ray; a holiday sounded okay to her, but getting her passport caused her to worry, none the less she answered the question with a happy tone to her voice, "Spain I think," she replied and then rolled on top of her 'Sir Galahad'.

Lizzie's thirst for revenge, with the bounty now placed on the head of her brother's killer, had returned. Another visit to the boozer where she'd met Ron got her the address of 'Big H's' office, and a visit to him gave her some information that could be helpful.

"Ron's missus ain't been seen since he was shot and rumour has it that she could be with your brother's killer." 'Big H' looked at the slip of a girl in front of him and laughed.

"What's so funny?" Lizzie was upset by the fat bastard's attitude.

"Nothing, nothing really, but I can see a funny side. The bloke's called Ray and he's a professional hitman, do you really think you're gonna take him out."

Lizzie stared straight at 'Big H' with hate in her eyes. "And when I have, I'll pick up the reward money." She turned and walked out of the office, holding a piece of paper. It contained Ray's phone number. She was the second person, 'Big H' had given it to, and this time for free. "Poor girl," he thought. "She'll be going the same way as her brother, how the fuck could I charge her."

Lizzie now had some useful information and already

knew where Ron lived. She would pay the house a visit in the hope that both Ray and Ron's missus would be there. If that proved negative, then she'd phone the bastard; what she'd say she didn't know, but she had time to think about that. Back to see Claire first, though, she needed a gun and hoped her boss could help her.

"Best we go to your place at night I think" Ray was busy running his fingers over Brenda's body, "tonight, I think." Ray pulled away and jumped out of bed, "I'm gonna have a shower now."

Brenda's hurt expression turned into a smile when Ray held out his hand. "Coming with me?"

She climbed over the bed and then took hold of his hand, and stark-naked, they walked to the bathroom together.

Lizzie told Claire of her intentions. "I think you're bonkers young lady but I guess I ain't gonna persuade you to give this up." The boss gave Lizzie the revolver she wanted, "Let's hope they ain't there when she gets to the house." Claire was not happy with what she had just done.

CHAPTER 23

There wasn't a lot of conversation to be had as Ray and Brenda made the drive to the house she had shared with Ron. Ray was concentrating on the job in hand, something he would normally do without a distraction; Brenda was just plain shit-scared of this trip going pear-shaped. Ray parked the car away from the house, but with a clear view of it, no vehicles were parked on the drive or on the road outside, so Ray got out of his motor and took the front door key that Brenda had given him out of his pocket, she had another key in her purse, "Wait here, I won't be long." Ray patted his jacket and felt the gun and silencer in the pocket before setting off towards the house. He walked straight past, but slowly, looking for any signs of activity, he didn't see any, so turned back and walked up to the door. He opened it using his left hand; the pistol was in his right one, Ray turned the key slowly, and he hoped quietly before pushing the door open and entering the hallway. Brenda had told Ray that her passport was in the top drawer of a unit in the living room and the door to that room was straight in front of him. He closed the front door with great care and stood listening for a while; all he could hear was the ticking of a clock on the wall to his left next to the coat rail. The seconds passed by, he stayed still and continued to listen for any sound until he was happy that he was alone in the house; however, he kept his finger on the trigger of the gun as he walked towards the door and took hold of the handle while pressing the side of his head to the door at the same time, he continued to listen for any sounds of movement from within until he was happy that nobody was in the room. He slowly eased the handle down and opened the door but did not enter straight away. Met with a stony silence, he moved cautiously into the lounge, his 'minces' taking in the view of the furniture. Happy that he was alone, he walked in and made his way to the unit where he opened the top drawer; it was then that Ray heard a click and turned towards the door, his eyes opened wide in disbelief, "But I killed you."

The slip of a girl looked at him and laughed, "You thought you did, but you didn't check." Lizzie aimed the gun at Ray's body; I won't be making the same mistake. This is for my brother, you killed him, and now I'm gonna kill you."

At that moment, they both heard a key in the front door, Lizzie turned as Brenda entered, and Ray grabbed his chance and shot Lizzie for the second time, Lizzie pulled her trigger simultaneously, and her bullet buried itself in Brenda. Both women collapsed; Ray moved forward and put another bullet in Lizzie before moving to Brenda and dropping to his knees.

"Fuck, fuck, fuck, fuck, fuck, why didn't you wait in the motor?"

Brenda looked up at him, and as she spoke, blood began to trickle out of her mouth. "You was… such… a … long…"

Ray watched her eyes glaze over as she breathed her last few breaths, and then he heard footsteps outside. "It's only one person." He tucked himself behind the front door and waited for the intruder to pass into the hallway, Lizzie's gun wasn't fitted with a silencer, and now some nosey bastard was sticking his beak in where it wasn't wanted.

"Oh my God!" The intruder entered the house and took in the sight of the two women horizontal and leaking loads of claret, he dropped to his knees beside both bodies, and as he did so, Ray pulled the trigger for the third time. The bullet tore a hole in the back of the bloke's head, and he toppled forward like a felled tree. Ray stepped forward and put a second bullet in the intruder's body before stepping past the three corpses and out on to the drive; looking left and right, he saw nobody on the street, so he removed the silencer from his gun and put both parts back in his pocket, he walked away from the house and the three corpses at a fair pace, moments later he was sitting behind the wheel of his motor with tears escaping down both his cheeks, "Oh Brenda! Why didn't you stay in the car?" Ray wiped the tears away with his jacket sleeve, sat up straight, started the motor and left the scene. It was going to be a long and lonely drive back to the east coast for him.

Claire looked at the clock and sighed, "Where the fuck is she, the little bitch should be back by now." Nasty thoughts were buzzing around in Claire's head like a swarm of demented flies, and she wanted to scream out in a mixture of anger and desperation. She went to the drinks cabinet and poured herself a large neat vodka; as the first mouthful of drink hit the back of her throat, it made her shudder; the second mouthful didn't nor did the refill. Claire walked to the phone and lifted the receiver; moments later, 'Big H' answered, and after a short conversation, Claire replaced the receiver and returned to the drinks cabinet.

It was one long, exasperating hour before 'Big H' returned the call, a loud "Bollocks!" escaped from Claire's lips and then she slammed the phone down and threw her glass of vodka at the wall, "the stupid fuckin' little girl." Claire walked to her settee and plonked her arse down on it, and began to cry.

The 'Old Bill' were back at Ron's house after an anonymous tip-off and found the three corpses inside, "Bollocks, now we've got to get involved, fuck you Ron, who'd wanna pop your missus and who are the other two bloody corpses?"

The DCI pulled out a packet of fags and lit one up; he inhaled the smoke and then blew it out of his beak." Hours of fuckin' paperwork to look forward to now."

The triple murder and Ron's made that night's TV and the front pages of the following day's newspapers. Ray bought a copy of one from the newsagent and then walked to the same café that he and Brenda had sat and had breakfast every day during their short-lived relationship.

"On your own today pal, where's the other half?" the café owner enquired.

Ray looked back at the front page of the newspaper he was holding and then back up at the owner.

"Err! Yeah umm! Breakfast and a mug of tea." Ray turned and made his way to a table.

"Chatty little bastard." The owner kept his thoughts to himself and made his way to the kitchen. "One breakfast coming up and a mug of tea."

It was time for Ray to move on, so he finished his full English and went back to the rental, where he put everything into a bag and left. "New address and new look again." Ray sighed at the thought. He would grow a beard and moustache, crop his hair and then put some coloured contact lenses in.

His thoughts returned to the cute little Brenda, and what might have been had she waited in the car like he told her. "Bollocks."

He was brought back to the present by the ringing of his second phone; he pulled over off the road and answered it.

"What the fuck are you up to son? That's four bodies now and I guess you popped all of 'em, why?" It was 'Big

H', and he didn't sound too happy.

"The little prossie you shot at Ron's gaff was the sister of the bloke you shot in the 'carzy' at the pub but why did you pop Ron and then his missus, and who was the other geezer?"

"I didn't shoot Brenda, we were fucking off together for a new start, the other bird shot her and…"

"Are you off your trolley or what, running away together, you're not a couple of fuckin' love struck teenagers you silly bastard."

Big H's voice had risen with every word of the question he had asked, he was obviously unhappy with Ray's confession, and the reply he was about to receive did not please him either. "Listen Harry, it's a mess I'll give you that but it will all calm down I'm sure."

"Calm down, did you say, calm down, you stupid fuck," 'Big H's' voice continued to rise, and by the time the fuck left his lips, he was shrieking, but it returned to normal for his next sentence, "By the way there's a price on your fuckin' head so you need to lay low for a while."

Ray ended the call, and that didn't please 'Big H' either; he swore down the receiver before placing it back in its cradle. Ray was also pissed off now and big-time, just like his employer. Brenda was gone, and he had just become target practice for a load of greedy bastards that would all be trying to cash in on that reward.

Now that word was out about the four murders, it wouldn't take long before witnesses came forward, and a photofit was put together, and then Ray's mug would also be on the front page of most, if not all of the daily rags as well. Although nobody had actually seen him kill any of them, plenty of witnesses had watched him spanking the big ugly minder in the boozer, and all four victims had been found at the big bastard's house so Ray would be guilty of all the murders as far as the police were concerned, plus there were plenty of people that had seen Brenda and Ray together, linking him further to the murders. Hotel workers, pub staff, restaurant staff, the café owner. The list went on, and the need to change his identity now became a priority. The next question he asked himself was how many people had 'Big H' given his phone number to; while he had that phone, he could be traced, so he needed to rid himself of it; Ray smashed the bloody thing to pieces and binned it.

CHAPTER 24

The DCI in charge of the murder cases was Joe Brown, he'd grown up being ribbed about his name because of the singer with the same one, "No I ain't got no bruvvers, just two sisters" was something he told plenty of people when teased about the name of the singers backing group.

He was two years away from his pension and didn't want or need the amount of hard graft that would accompany this case. He was holding court at the Police Station; those there had all been busy chatting idly when he walked in. A cough and an "okay listen up you lot" gained the small entourages' attention.

"Okay, first Ron was shot, no great loss by any stretch of the imagination and I was hoping to wrap the case up a bit lively, even sweep it under the carpet and then some silly bastard, and it was probably the same one that killed Ron seeing as it was at the same address, goes and gives us another three corpses." DCI Brown exhaled heavily and took out a packet of cigarettes from the top pocket of his suit jacket and lit up; he inhaled the smoke and then slowly blew it out before continuing.

"We know that one of the three corpses was Ron's missus so we need names for the other two and a motive. I don't need this case to drag on for ages so lets get out and get some answers. We also need a name and a face for the killer."

The other coppers exchanged looks, but nobody made a move.

"What's the matter with you lot, get out and talk to all your informants and any other low life 'crim' you know. Somebody will know something." A minute later, Joe was on his own.

The bloke found on Ron's floor was identified quickly, and a background check informed DCI Brown that he had no record, nor it would seem any connection to the hood or his missus.

"So why was he there? I need answers."

The girl was proving a bit harder to trace. "Somebody knows who she is, so keep asking."

DCI Brown was drinking a coffee and puffing on a fag when one of his team burst into his office.

"Guv, we've just had a call from a café owner on the east coast, he's got a place just outside of Yarmouth, anyway he recognised that Brenda bird from the front page of the papers and rang to say she was a regular in his café with some geezer, been having breakfast there every morning for the last couple of weeks. They were a real loved up pair according to him, except that the other day the geezer turned up on his own."

Joe looked at the copper in front of him, "Well done, you got an address?"

"Yes Guv."

"Good, then let's get down there and get a description of this bloke who was with her, I'm guessing he's our killer."

DCI Brown finished his coffee and threw the beaker in the bin; he took a last drag on the fag and stubbed it out on the overflowing ashtray that sat on his desktop. Grabbing his coat, he made his way out of the room with the copper close on his heels. A couple of hours later, and after a meal washed down with a mug of tea kindly provided by the café owner, DCI Brown and his sidekick were heading back to the station armed with a description. The café owner had agreed to call in to the station that evening to help put together a photofit.

The next morning DCI Brown was made aware of the spanking Ron had received; a couple of witnesses had come forward with a description of the assailant that matched the one he'd received regarding the bloke that spent a couple of weeks with Brenda.

"We're getting somewhere now but it's far from sorted so keep up the good work." The coppers left the station, and Joe was alone once again.

"So, this bloke pops Ron and has it on his toes with the missus, they were all loved up according to the café owner, so why has she turned up 'brown bread' and how are the other two corpses connected?"

DCI Brown left his office and made his way to the car park. "I need to pay 'Big H' a visit; if anybody knows anything worth knowing, it will be him.

DCI Joe Brown left 'Big H's' office wearing a grin; a threat of swarming his office with the 'Old Bill' had forced him to part with some useful information. His next stop was Claire's house, and a bit more info from the madam had the case moving along at a fair pace. The photofit of Ray had been pretty near the mark, and when it was made public, a whole load of bounty hunters were rubbing their hands together; the race for Ray's scalp was now on.

A post mortem informed the DCI that two guns had been used at the murder scene and that Ray had probably not been responsible for Brenda's murder, but all three corpses had been shot at the same time. Joe Brown paid Claire another visit to ask why Lizzie would want Brenda dead, "there is no reason that I know of." The DCI left empty-handed.

"So maybe this other squeaky clean bloke is responsible

for her death but he has no reason to kill her and appears to have been an innocent casualty."

He'd been given a name, had a job, a family and had been on his way home from work. "A wrong place, wrong time" casualty. Claire had not recognised Ray as a customer, so a love triangle scenario between Ray, Brenda and Lizzie had been ruled out.

Several weeks passed, long ones for the DCI and his crew, with no sightings of Ray. A background check on Lizzie had revealed her troubled past but still hadn't provided a reason for her wanting Brenda dead.

DCI Joe Brown lit up a fag and poured himself a single malt, "This case ain't getting wrapped up anytime soon. He blew out the smoke he'd just inhaled, downed the drink in one and walked out of the office. A loud "Bollocks" escaped from his lips as he closed the door.

CHAPTER 25

Ray was pretty certain that he was safe. He had changed his identity and ditched his phones once he'd written down any useful numbers; they included 'Big H's'. He'd laid low in Scotland for a while, remote and safe, but he wanted to return South and hoped that things had quietened down. Ray had kept asking himself why Lizzie had put a bullet in Brenda, and the only answer he came up with was that she must have panicked when the door opened. He was certain that the two didn't know each other even though Lizzie had been with Ron the night he had ended that thug's reign of terror. "She panicked, there ain't no other explanation."

He left Scotland driving a second hand Ford Escort that he'd bought for cash and hoped it would make the journey which was the length of the A1 and then some, part one of that wish came true when he drove in to London, familiar territory for him, but once there he was uncertain of his next move. On impulse, he drove to 'Big H's' and walked into his office.

"Can I help you son?"

Ray was happy that he had not been recognised and smiled, "I'm looking for a bit of work Harry, got anything for me?"

'Big H' was taken aback by the new appearance that accompanied the familiar voice.

"Fuckin' hell son, I didn't recognise ya, but you must be off your trolley coming back here, the 'Old Bill' have been sniffing around and are keen to have a word with ya and fuck knows how many people want your scalp, there's a decent price being offered for that bit of merchandise.

"I know all that but laying low gets boring and I could do with boosting my funds, so do you have anything?"

"I do as it happens Ray, how do I make contact with you?"

Harry was wearing a smile that carried no warmth.

"You don't, get everything together for me and I'll be in touch with you." Ray left the office.

Harry sat behind his desk with his elbows on top and little podgy fingers locked, "What's my next move." He unlocked his fingers and opened a drawer; taking out a bottle of whisky, he poured himself a shot and drank it straight down. He returned the bottle and glass to the drawer and then picked up the phone.

Ray walked into the room he'd just booked at a Bed and Breakfast and lay down on the bed. A look around the room told him that his digs weren't five star, a single bed, cabinet, and wardrobe was the only furniture, and they were all tired looking, but it would do, for now, it wasn't too bad on the wallet, and the owner didn't want too much information from him. He needed a new passport and would call in on the counterfeiter that he knew tomorrow and organise that before parking up outside 'Big H's' office to watch who was going in and out before calling in and collecting the paperwork for his next hit if there was one.

Claire put the receiver back on the phone and allowed herself a smile before picking it back up and making a call. The line of business that she was in meant she knew a few nasty geezers that she employed from time to time to sort any customers that gave her girls any grief.

"Antonio, I have some work for you."

The pair replaced their receivers in unison, and an hour later, Antonio walked into the brothel that Claire owned. Standing upright, the Italian stood 6ft 3in tall and weighed in at eighteen and a half stone, he was a big lump but carried no fat, and his features looked like they'd been chiselled from a block of stone. A full head of jet black hair sat atop those features and possessed a parting that was dead straight. He would have looked at home in any mafia film, especially as he was wearing his black suit, white shirt, tie and highly polished black shoes. After a short conversation with Claire and a complimentary shag with one of her girls, Antonio left the brothel, he would be spending the next day at 'Big H's' office. Ray was parked up opposite when the Italian made his entry; he sat up in his seat, pulled open the glove compartment and took out his piece, attaching the silencer he put it in the holder he was wearing under his jacket and walked across the road, Ray waited a couple of minutes before walking in. Big H' and Antonio were the only two in the office, and as he opened the door, 'H' greeted him by saying his name loudly, "Ray, good to see you again."

Ray's eyes were focussed on the big Italian who stuck his hand inside his jacket and grabbed his pistol, but Ray was a split second ahead of his wannabe assassin and pumped two bullets straight into his heart. The big man fell to the floor with a look of surprise on his face, the faster man had gained victory, and the look had seemed to be in recognition of that fact as Antonio hit the floor. The colour had drained from 'Big H's' 'boat', and he couldn't mask the look of fear that was spread across it. Ray turned his gun on him and smiled a very satisfied smile.

"I should pop you next for trying to pull that stroke, Harry." The look of fear was now accompanied by a begging one, "Give me one good reason why I shouldn't."

Harry opened his mouth and tried to speak, but nothing

came out; Ray laughed and moved to within arm's reach of the little fat man, he pushed the nozzle of his gun against 'Big H's' temple and heard the little whimper that escaped his lips, Ray followed the man's gaze down to his crutch and let out a laugh, "Had a little accident Harry?"

The wet patch in his trousers answered the question without Harry having to speak.

"I ain't gonna shoot you," a look of relief replaced the one of fear, "but you're gonna pay me double whatever you were paying that big lump and then some, okay."

'Big H' still couldn't speak, so he nodded with a frenzied action and took out a wad of £50 notes from the drawer; Ray kept the gun pointed at his head and took the money out of his hand before backing his way out of the office, Harry hadn't wanted to pay Ray the whole wad and was going to count out a few of the notes, he'd just been mugged and once he was gone the hood let out a staccato sigh before banging his fists down on his desk. "You really are a dead man walking now you mug."

Ray now had a nice few readies to add to the stash he'd brought with him, but his new identity had been compromised, and he needed to change it again. Hair colour and cut, colour of eyes which meant new contact lenses and shaving off the goatee he'd grown. He would stay in London though, just keep a low profile for a while. Knowing he'd pissed 'Big H' off was a cause for concern, the man had contacts and money, and the bounty on Ray's head had probably just increased by a fair margin.

"Maybe I should turn myself in, could do with the rest, although 'life' would mean quite a few years, fuck it! I'll just have to sort things." But he didn't have a 'scooby' as to how he would do that. "I'll come up with something, I'm sure."

When 'Big H' informed Claire that Antonio was no more, thanks to Ray, the woman was a bit more than hacked off. He left out the bit about pissing himself when he told her how it happened but admitted to losing quite a few quid when Ray grabbed the money out of his hand while holding a gun to his head.

"We both have our reasons for wanting him dead now." Claire replaced the receiver and went to the drinks cabinet, where she poured herself a large vodka with just a splash of orange. "Fuck you Ray!" The aggrieved woman downed the drink and then poured another. 'Big H' had told her about the changes to his features; he told quite a few people but didn't hold out much hope that he would retain that look for much longer. He was right, of course, and Ray had added a small 'mars bar' to his right cheek for good effect. His false passport, along with a driving licence, was in the process of being made, and the hitman was feeling happier. He'd signed out of the B and B where he was staying and then, after carrying out the changes to his looks, booked back in again with a new name. The manager had not recognised him, but that didn't mean too much as the bloke hadn't paid too much attention either time he'd booked in.

"What's your next move son?"

Ray put the question to himself but wasn't too sure of the answer. "Holiday abroad? Move back up North? Stay where you are and find some work? Fucked if I know to be honest."

Ray decided to find a quiet boozer and weigh up his options while enjoying a couple of pints. The Nags Head fitted that bill, and he parked himself on a seat away from the bar but facing the door. Ray liked his back to a wall and to be able to see who came and went, an old habit of his that made him feel safe; he unfolded his newspaper and started to read.

Half an hour later, Ray was on his second pint of lager when the place started to fill up. Most of the new customers looked like white-collar workers, but a couple were clearly builders; there were only a few women. Ray looked at each and every one of them and decided that no one posed a threat. Why would they, it was a new look Ray that was enjoying his pint, and nobody knew him, but habit made him check everybody anyway.

Two blokes parked their arses on seats by him and put their beers on his table; they leaned into one another and started talking. Their voices were only just above a whisper; Ray was interested in what they had to say; why? He wasn't sure, but they were the only two in the Nags Head that weren't loud. Intrigued, Ray continued to listen while perusing the newspaper, turning the page every so often but not really reading anything. Both blokes were booted and suited, and looking at their hands, Ray guessed neither had ever taken part in a day's manual labour, they were both clean-shaven too, and Ray could smell their aftershaves; their conversation was completely out of keeping with their looks. Ray continued to listen with an interest that was growing with each sentence. Neither of them struck Ray as being 'tea leafs' but here they were planning to rob their workplace, and they were talking large numbers, Ray fancied half inching the money for himself. How could these two stop him, "Easy money son, easy money."

Ray digested all the information before 'necking' the rest of his pint, folding up his paper and quietly leaving the bar. He checked his watch and reckoned he had time for a kip before a shower and a shave, then armed with his gun and knuckle dusters, he'd fleece these two office boys.

Four hours later, the nozzle of Ray's gun was resting against the left temple of one of the unlikely lads, and as the catch went back, it triggered a reaction from the poor bastard's bladder. Just like 'Big H' had done when he was threatened with a gun, the bloke pissed himself, the reaction amused Ray, "Give him the bag John, please give him the bag." The words were said in a whimper that was filled with fear. John looked undecided, and so Ray pulled the trigger, John's accomplice fell to the floor, and John screamed out in anger, "No, this is not how it happens." He swung the bag at Ray's head, but the mugger was ready and grabbing it with his left hand, he pulled John off balance and towards him, letting go of the bag Ray smashed a left hook into the side of John's head, but he wasn't giving up that easy, "You Bastard," the words carried a venom that Ray was sure didn't normally exist in the bloke's make-up and the following swing of the bag, packed with the takings, hit Ray with a force that knocked him over. John kicked out at Ray's body, screaming with anger at the same time, he then kicked out again, but this time Ray caught his foot and twisted it; John toppled to the floor but hung on to the bag. A pull of the trigger and the grip was released; John had just joined his workmate, the latest person to fall foul of Ray's Glock G2B. Ray put the gun back in his jacket and picked up the bag. "That was fucking easy." There was a spring in his step as he made his way back to his digs.

Pulling the trigger still excited Ray, as did seeing someone's face fall apart when smashed with a set of knuckle dusters, 'Sick Bastard' was how he described himself; it was a fact that was difficult to prove wrong, but now that he was minted he could walk away from all that, retire somewhere sunny where nobody knew him and start again. "I don't think I can," he told himself "this violence is a drug to me, could be alcohol or cocaine, heroin even, but no, I had to become addicted to violence."

The two latest deaths that he'd added to his ever-growing list and the big financial gain he'd just inherited left Ray feeling horny; he needed a brothel so that he could 'unload', and so he went in search of one. The madam was a tidy little bit but not available, "I've got enough money to make you change your mind." The brothel owner looked at him and smiled, "I told you I'm not on the menu at any price, so please just pick one of the girls that are." The request was delivered with a smile, and so Ray sighed and put his money on the counter before setting off with a little redhead that had more than her fair share of bust, the skirt she was wearing also struggled to contain her well-rounded arse. The girl led Ray away, and he patted that arse as he followed her. The sex that took place was heavy duty with first Ray on top, then the redhead before the climax came with Ray fucking her doggie fashion, they climaxed together, something that didn't happen too often for the prostitute, and as he left the room, she kissed him on the cheek and asked for another visit in the not too distant future. Ray smiled and left the brothel, a happy man. The coming weeks would see Ray 'banging' the little redhead on a regular basis, so much so that the madam pulled him to one side and suggested he try one of the other girls. When Ray had refused, he received a warning that if he tried to make his visits about anything other than sex, things could get nasty for him. Ray had laughed at the madam, "She's hardly wedding material, but if you want me to fuck somebody else the offer I made you is still there for the taking."

Ray had carried on banging the redhead. He also kept an eye on 'Big H's' office. It amused him to see most of the blokes that passed in and out dressed the same, dark blue 'whistle' white shirt, black tie, Crombie coat and highly polished black shoes. He imagined them all as actors auditioning for a gangster movie. It also tickled him that he attributed an American accent to each and every one of them. "Too many Edward G Robinson movies I guess."

It was a Wednesday afternoon, a miserable day with a grey sky and a cold, damp feel to the air; Ray wished it was warmer and was thinking of calling it a day when his bottom jaw dropped, and his 'minces' nearly popped out of his head.

"What the fuck would she be doing with 'Big H'" he

asked himself. It was the madam from the brothel, "Maybe paying him protection money, can't think of any other connection. Oh! To be a fly on his office wall right now."

Unbeknown to Ray, Claire had entered the office armed with a photograph of him and put it on 'Big H's' desk. The little fat man studied it for an age.

"Well," Claire asked, "do you know him or not."

Harry kept looking and did not reply.

"Say something for fuck's sake, you know him don't you, I can tell. Wanna tell me who he is and if I should be worried or not."

The silence that was returned started to niggle Claire, "Say something… please," Claire slammed the palm of her hand on to the desk, and Harry looked up with a start, "well, are you gonna tell me who the fuck he is please?"

"I can't be sure Claire but I think it's the hit man that took care of your Lizzie."

The madam was taken aback, "What d'ya mean you can't be sure? Either it is or it isn't which one is it?"

Harry looked up; the bloke's a chameleon Claire, keeps changing his appearance but the height and build look about right; the scar on his kisser is new, though.

"Maybe it ain't real", Claire offered.

"Maybe, I'll have to call round when he is next there, his voice won't have changed."

"I'll call you Harry."

Claire left the office; Ray was intrigued as to why she had been there, "What's the connection?" he asked himself, "it might be me!" He intended to find out.

CHAPTER 26

'Big H's' door flew open, and the little fat man sat up with a start as Ray entered with his gun aimed straight at him, the poor bastard's bladder gave way again, and he cursed. It was Ray, the man fitted the photo complete with the newly acquired scar on his 'boat', he didn't need to speak, Harry knew it was him. Ray walked over to Harry and rested the nozzle of the gun against the fat man's temple; some more piss escaped 'Big H's' bladder, causing the man's face to go a deep red colour."

"I guess you've just pissed yourself again big man," Ray laughed, "tell me your connection with the bird from the brothel and I'll let you live, but tell me the truth, I don't wanna hear a load of bollocks from ya! Do you understand?"

Ray pushed the nozzle into the side of Harry's head and his bladder leaked a little bit more.

"Fuck you, take the gun away and we can talk." Harry was now uncomfortable in his warm, wet trousers and wanted to change them but knew he couldn't move while he had this nutter in his office pressing the gun into his head, oh! How he wished somebody would remove this itch and collect the reward, but it wasn't going to happen on this visit and 'Big H' needed rid of him so that he could shower and change his clothes.

"She called in to pay the protection money due."

"I don't think so Harry; you'd have had it collected from her, maybe even driven over to her and collected it yourself to maybe even fitting in a shag while you were there, I take it your little todger still works, or is it just for pissing out of these days? Something you seem to be doing regularly now even though it's still in your trousers." Ray laughed at his own little joke, but Big H didn't see the funny side of it and continued to scowl at his unwanted guest. He pushed the nozzle of his gun harder against the big man's temple, and a bit more piss escaped the poor bastard's bladder; he felt ready to explode with anger but stayed calm for fear of being shot.

"The fucking payment was late and so she brought it round in person, I ain't fucking lying you bastard, now get that fucking gun away from my fucking head."

Ray pulled the gun back and Harry's frame relaxed, a second later the butt of the gun slammed into the side of his head, and Harry lost consciousness. Ray pushed his chair back from the desk and opened the top drawer. He took the photo and turned it over. "You lying bastard." Ray turned and whipped the gun across 'Big H's' face, the skin under his left eye parted and blood started to pour out of the wound; the second blow was a backward swipe and ripped open the right eye. Ray then smashed the butt of the gun down on hapless Harry's beak and the bone gave way. With a hefty shove from Ray the chair toppled backwards, and the legs gave way. With his face smashed and his pants pissed the gangster was now lying in a heap on the floor; Ray walked over to the office door and locked it, he then pulled the blinds down on the windows and, taking a chair, he sat himself down by the hapless figure and waited.

It was a lengthy wait, but Ray had nowhere to go, and so he sat in Big H's office with an air of contentment about him. Finally, the little fat man moved and made a grunting noise, he thought he'd opened his 'minces' but found himself looking through two slits, he raised one of his podgy little hands to his face, it was wet, and when he looked through his two slits, he saw it was blood, his blood. Big H winced as he touched his swollen eyes, and a noise that was filled with pain escaped from his lips; he then touched his crotch and felt the wet piss on his trousers. A low 'fuck' escaped from his lips; he then realised he was lying on the floor. "What…"

"Welcome back you lying bastard." Ray walked over to Big H, stuck an arm under each armpit, and with immense effort, he pulled the rounded little lump upright; Ray then uprighted the chair and sat his victim on it before sucking in a large volume of air and exhaling slowly. Harry didn't speak.

"You're one heavy little fat bastard, Phew! Lifting you took some effort trust me, anyway you must be more comfortable now." Ray took in a few more deep breaths, releasing them slowly. "Now where were we, Oh yeah, you were just about to tell me what the madam from the brothel was doing here and don't give me any more of that protection money bollocks because I'll have to kill you if you lie again. Now we both know that it had nothing to do with paying her debt cos I found this photo in your drawer so start explaining and start now." Ray put the photo down on the desktop, and although he was struggling to see anything through the two slits that had replaced his eyes, he knew full well that Ray had taken the photo that Claire had given him out of the drawer of his desk. Harry took a hankie out of his pocket and made himself busy dabbing at his 'minces' and 'beak', wincing with every dab and failed to reply. Ray slammed the palm of his right hand down on the desk and caused Big H to flinch, not for the first time that day. "Start fucking talking, and start now or I'll hurt you some more you bastard."

Big H coughed to clear his throat, and a blood-splattered spray escaped from his lips.

"Fuck, I'm in pain Ray, and loads of it, I need to go to hospital." Big H was pleading with his tormentor.

"What was that bitch here for?"

Ray hit the desk for a second time and caused Big H to wince again and pull back from him.

"Start fucking talking or I'll start inflicting more pain before I pull the trigger and put an end to all your misery you bastard."

"Okay, okay." A big sigh followed the two words, and then Harry told the truth while Ray sat and took it all in. At the end of the confession Harry begged Ray to take him to hospital. Ray stood up and unlocked the door before walking out of the office, letting the door slam shut behind him. Now on his own, Big H suddenly felt broken and started to cry. Ray drove to his 'digs'; he needed time to take in what he'd just learned and the connection between all the past events. He'd taken out a brother and a sister and pissed off the brothel owner but still didn't understand why Lizzie had killed Brenda. Next stop for Ray had to be the brothel and confront Claire before Harry told her that the photo was definitely him.

The tears of self-pity had finally stopped, and Harry pulled himself up out of the chair and made his way to the bathroom at the back of the office. He stood at the mirror above the sink and cleaned off the blood as best he could looking through the slits that were now his eyes and cleared the blood from his nostrils, wincing with every touch. The gangster had just taken a good hiding, and it was painful, but the biggest pain was being emitted from his dented ego. "Revenge Harry, we need revenge." He told himself before taking his clothes off and walking into the shower where he stood under the running water for an age, just letting the water run over him. "You pissed yourself again, I can't fucking believe that you pissed your pants for a second time." Big H was now angry with himself and slapped his cheek, causing himself more pain; self-pity and anger were now fighting each other. A second slap from anger caused him to cry out in pain and self-pity walked in at this point and claimed victory. A very disconsolate being walked out of the shower and wrapped himself in his dressing-gown, "I need a fucking drink." The crestfallen figure made his way to his desk, where he opened the drawer and took out a glass and the bottle of single malt. He would now soak his pain and misery in a large volume of alcohol. It would ease the pain, and after the recovery, which was not going to happen overnight, he would go about seeking revenge and having Ray taken out. The hitman's actions had caused the bounty on him to double again.

CHAPTER 27

Detective Chief Inspector Joe Brown was at the scene of the two dead office workers; he was scratching his head and at a loss as to why they had been popped. He pulled out wallets from their jackets; credit cards and cash were in both.

"They weren't mugged, so why are they dead?"

A quick check on the phone informed Joe that the two men worked together and were only yards from their workplace, further enquiries told him that a large sum of money had gone missing from their workplace and DCI Brown assumed these two had stolen it and then somebody had mugged them after that, but not for the contents of their wallets, that was small change compared to the sum that had gone missing. The autopsy threw another spanner in the works for DCI Brown when he was informed that the gun used to kill these two latest corpses was the same one used to pop Ron, Lizzie and the 'nosey bollocks'.

Back at the office the DCI asked himself another question 'how the fuck are these lot connected?' Joe Brown scratched his head and poured himself a large single malt. "I really don't need this shit." The whisky disappeared from the glass with one swallow.

CHAPTER 28

The front door of the brothel opened and Claire looked up to see Ray walking in, she pushed a button on the desk and two big burly geezers appeared by her side. Ray smiled, "Is my regular shag available?"

"You know which room she's in."

Ray put his money on the table, and Claire smiled; the hitman returned the compliment and then looked the two geezers up and down, their physiques were pretty impressive and their 'boat races' wore 'don't mess with us stares' or maybe they said: "Do mess with us and we'll enjoy tearing you apart." Ray turned away from them and walked down the passage to the prostitute's room.

"He's the one that killed my top earning girl, I don't think he's aware of that fact but I can't take any chances that's why you two are here, there's a big chunk of money being offered for his scalp."

The two heavies nodded at Claire and made their way down to the room where Ray was; they stood outside and waited for the grunts to begin before walking in. Ray heard the handle go down and pulled out of his whore. It only took him seconds to pull up his trousers and turn round. The whore pulled the sheets up and over her head; she didn't move or peep out. Ray turned towards his attackers but didn't have time to pull his knuckle dusters or his pistol out before a meaty sized fist slammed into the side of his head and sent him sprawling and, as he hit the deck, two pairs of hands grabbed him and pulled him to his feet. Another blow slammed into his stomach and caused him to cry out in pain; two more punches had him depositing his lunch on the bedroom floor. The two minders then dragged Ray out of the room and down the passage to a waiting Claire.

"Well now Ray, I think that's what you're calling yourself at the moment, I will be making a phone call in a minute and collecting a nice sum of money as I hand you over to Robert who wants you for killing his sidekick Ron and fucking his sidekick's missus, Brenda. You also fucked things up a little bit for me when you took out my top earner after she shot Brenda. You've upset quite a few people including Big H who is still smarting from the beating you gave him and now it's payback time. Oh! Yeah and Harry, God bless him, has doubled that bounty."

Ray never said a word or tried to break free from the two minders who were holding him in a vice-like grip, but it was obvious to him that he needed to do something and fairly quickly as he wasn't ready to meet his maker just yet. He watched Claire disappear down the passageway and, a couple of minutes later, return carrying a set of handcuffs. The minders forced his arms behind his back, and Claire slapped the cuffs on before fetching a chair and putting it behind him. The pressure on his shoulders was immense, and he had no other option but to sit on the chair. The madam then made her way to the phone and arranged to have the hitman exchanged for the large sum of money that had been placed on his head.

"Happy days Ray, fuck knows what this bloke's gonna do to you but for the money he's paying I'd say you're in for a lot of pain, Ouch!" Claire pursed her lips and blew a kiss in Ray's direction, "the money is gonna go a long way to healing the pain you caused when you took Lizzie away from me."

Ray looked at Claire and smiled, "Want some real money lady, if you let me go I can pay you a lot more than you're about to collect for handing me over to this Robert."

Claire looked at Ray for a moment and returned the smile. "Maybe what I'm about to collect is enough and the thought of you suffering before you're removed from this planet, well that might just be priceless, I might even ask if I can come along and watch." Claire placed her hand on her crutch and rubbed gently, "You might just make me cum without the shag."

Claire took her hand off her crutch and then lifted it to her mouth where she licked her index finger and then laughed; she blew Ray another kiss. "And anyway, if I don't hand you over Robert is gonna be pissed off big time, who knows what he'll do" Claire turned and went to walk away.

"Hang on, hang on just a minute please", there was a matter of urgency in Ray's voice that caused the madam to turn and face him, "You can say I got away and give him the address where I'm staying as a lead. Sure he'll be pissed off but he can then come after me himself. If he gets hold of me you can still cop the reward and what I give you, winner, winner, what do you say?"

"And if you get the better of him?"

"I'll take what money he's got on him and give it to you."

"And why would you do that?"

"I wanna stay alive, that's why". The strength of the plea in Ray's voice had grown to such a level that it made Claire laugh.

"My, you really are sounding desperate Ray."

The two minders hadn't released their grip, and they were causing Ray considerable pain, another reason for his voice going up an octave.

Claire turned her attention to the two of them. "What do you think boys, should I spare the poor bastard or not?"

Their grips strengthened, and a painful groan escaped from Ray's lips. Claire laughed again, and at that moment Ray wanted to take the bitch out, but he couldn't. His tease walked over and undid the cuffs she had put on him. "Okay we have a deal". The minders released their grips, and Ray let a sigh escape from his lips as he stood up; Claire walked round to face him and moving close, she grabbed his manhood and squeezed hard, causing Ray to squeal, her accompanying laugh had Ray close to exploding with anger but the two hefty bastards either side of him caused him to refrain from doing anything rash. Claire released her grip and then caressed the area softly; she looked at Ray as she ran her tongue across her top lip and, despite the pain, his cock started to harden. Claire felt the reaction and made a licking action with her tongue. Ray was now in possession of an erection; he wasn't a happy boy, he was a lot less happy when Claire clenched her fist and punched him in the bollocks, a painful sound escaped from Ray's lips, and Claire laughed as he collapsed to his knees.

"Pick him up boys and go collect the money, if he tries anything shoot him and bring his body back."

Ray was lifted to his feet and marched from the property.

Robert was not exactly smiling when he arrived at Claire's brothel and was told Ray was no longer there; however, his facial expression changed when the madam gave him the hitman's address. As he and his two minders went to leave, Claire asked for the reward money.

"Have I go the bastard yet, no, so I won't be paying you just yet. If he's where you say he is and he becomes my property then I'll be back with the money."

Robert smiled at Claire, "However, if it all goes tits up and he gets away I'll be back and for obvious reasons you'll not be happy to see me."

Robert's smile disappeared, and the three men made their way outside.

Claire poured herself a large G and T and sat down. When the two minders returned with a holdall stuffed with banknotes, her mince pies lit up, and the frown she was wearing after Robert's visit was replaced by a big smile.

"I need you boys to hang around for a while if that's okay." Brenda passed a bundle of dough to each of them and then passed them a condom each. "Now go choose your bonus fuck, I ain't expecting any visitors for a while."

Claire walked to her living room and put the holdall in her safe.

Ray sat on a chair in the bedroom of his B and B and waited; forty minutes later Robert and his two minders arrived. Ray listened to their footsteps as they made their way up the flight of stairs and along the passageway to his door, they stopped outside and he listened to some mumbling before the door flew open and slammed against the wall. The two minders burst into the room; they were both armed, but Ray was ready, and two pulls of the trigger took them out of the game. Ray now stood up and looked straight at Robert standing in the doorway, his gun pointing straight at Ray.

"I didn't want it to end like this, I wanted you to feel pain and die slowly." Robert pulled the trigger three times as he climbed over the bodies blocking the doorway and entered the room.

"But an eye for an eye and all that bollocks." The gangster looked for Ray's body, but it wasn't on the floor, then he felt the cold metal against the side of his head, and he couldn't move, the trigger was pulled, and Robert was also removed from the planet. As the bullet went in, the blood sprayed out, and now Ray needed a shower and a change of clothes, but he also needed to make a sharp exit, have it on his toes before the 'old Bill' arrived.

He went through the pockets of the three corpses, lifting their wallets and the car keys before wiping the 'claret' from his 'boat' with a towel. The envelope he lifted from the inside pocket of Robert's jacket was stuffed with a wedge of notes, and Ray laughed once he realised he'd collected his own bounty money.

The noise the door had made being kicked open by one of the minders was heard by the owner of the B and B, but he wasn't a brave man and, having seen the size of the two men accompanying Robert and seeing the gangster himself, he'd decided to stay put and pour himself a brandy.

There was a look of total disbelief written all over his 'kisser' when Ray walked past him, and once he'd gone out of the front door, the owner rushed up the stairs to find the three corpses. "Oh Fuck!" he exclaimed as he turned and made his way back downstairs.

CHAPTER 29

Detective Chief Inspector Joe Brown looked at the three bodies and cursed; he was fairly certain that the report would confirm that the same gun had been used to waste this known villain that had been used to waste all the rest of the bodies on his patch. There was a connection between Robert, the two burly goons and Ron; Brenda had been a casualty and Lizzie was somehow involved because she had shot Brenda; the two thieves were somehow connected, or were they? Joe wasn't sure, but the one thing he was sure about was the fact that he now had nine corpses on his hands and one dangerous man that needed catching and catching soon; he left one of his cops to get a description from the owner and walked out on to the street. Just up the road, he spotted a boozer, and that's where he went next. "Fuck, I need a drink, maybe even two".

CHAPTER 30

Ray needed another change of identity now and to lay low for a while; it was all getting a bit messy, and the prospect of a life behind bars wasn't really grabbing him or leaving him with a warm glow, but he had something to collect before he had it on his toes, so it was back to the brothel. "The perfect place," he told himself as he squeezed his erection through his trousers, "and two more corpses will be added to the list." Ray's smile grew as he squeezed his cock a bit harder and his smile turned into a laugh.

Claire thought about how easy it had been relieving Ray of the holdall and was now waiting for Robert to arrive and pay her the bounty she was due for giving him the hitman. She was very pleased with her day's work, but chickens had been counted prematurely, and when it was Ray, not Robert, that entered the brothel, her happiness was quickly punctured and deflated and unbeknown to her, Ray had already made an entry into the brothel via a prostitutes bedroom window. She wasn't by her counter or the panic button and, as she headed in that direction, Ray grabbed her and shoved a hand across her mouth; he marched her into the living room and closed the door, as she was pushed on to the sofa, the madam went to scream, but when Ray pointed a gun at her head she was too scared and remained silent. Ray kept the gun aimed at Claire, and she remained silent as he took out a roll of tape and used it to gag her; he then tied her hands behind her back. Ray stared at Claire, the eyes lacked any warmth, and he could see the fear that she felt at the possibility of losing her life in them, Ray smiled at her, and the look she then gave the hitman told him that she knew he was in charge and that she was one unhappy lady, Claire's expression changed again when Ray moved close and unbuttoned her blouse and pushing his hand behind her he undid her bra, Ray's smile stayed in place and it told Claire that he was about to enjoy what he was going to do to her, the madam's facial expression was full of anger.

The cord Ray had used to tie the madam up was stopping him from removing both items of clothing and so he untied her, a feeling of rage-filled Claire and overcame her fear from the gun, her angry expression remained as she swung her clenched right hand in Ray's direction, the blow was easily blocked, and the overly hard slap delivered to the side of her face brought her attack to a swift close and dumped her into a blackness.

It was several minutes before Claire opened her 'mince pies' again, and when the woman did, she was horrified to find herself naked and tied up once again. Claire looked up from her nakedness and saw Ray sitting opposite her with his gun aimed in her direction, "Nice tits lady", Ray laughed "but I want my money back before we have some fun."

The hatred Claire now felt for Ray was there to be seen in the stare she gave him; Ray continued, "I've taken your clothes off so that it's easier for you to do as I say without any more silly thoughts entering your head."

The cold stare continued, and Ray nodded. "I guess we're in agreement, now go to wherever it is you've put my money for safe keeping and bring it to me. I'm guessing you've hidden it in this room."

Claire stared towards the door, willing her two minders

to appear. Ray read her mind, "They're not gonna show I'm afraid, 'brown bread' the pair of 'em, the front doors locked and all the girls are a bit tied up at the moment." Ray laughed at his little joke; he then stood up and walked over to the naked figure, "I'm gonna untie you again but try anything silly and you'll be joining your two boys, understand?"

Claire nodded back in acceptance of the terms she'd received, and minutes later, the holdall was back in Ray's possession, and Claire's ties were back in place. Ray pressed the nozzle of his gun lightly between Claire's tits and moved it down her body, licking his lips at the same time, mimicking her actions from their last encounter. "Now when I first met you I offered to pay for a fuck and you turned me down, now I'm gonna help myself to a freebie even though my bollocks are a bit sore from your earlier actions." Claire let Ray do just that because she valued her life, but matters were made worse for her when she orgasmed before him; she hated herself for being aroused, but at least she was still taking in oxygen.

On a whim, Big H, although still wracked with pain, decided to call on Claire to see if Ray had been handed over to Robert. Now that he had provided the 'ol Bill', with a photo of the hitman and tipped off Claire that she would be getting a visit from the hitman, he decided he should receive a share of the spoils Robert had passed to her for Ray's scalp. His jaw dropped almost to the floor when he walked in and found Claire naked and tied up; he enjoyed both the view and untying her; she saw the mess his 'boat' was in but did not comment because she was too embarrassed by her state of undress, the madam told him what had happened to her, omitting the grand finale from her tale, it had been a decent fuck, and she'd had an orgasm, but Big H didn't need to know that. Claire was not shocked to find out that Ray was responsible for the gangster's injuries; he chose to leave out the part where he had pissed himself with fear when he regaled her with his tale of woe.

"The man's a fucking killing machine, something I used to my advantage on more than a few occasions but now he needs stopping before he tops one or both of us."

Claire nodded in agreement, "You've got some tasty geezers working for you 'H', surely you can have the bastard taken care of, he's already taken out three of my workers."

Big H was pissed off big time with Ray, he'd just stopped him from cashing in on his death, and it now looked like it would be costing him money to have him erased as he'd already doubled the bounty on offer. "Fuck this Claire, it's now gonna cost me a sizeable wedge of dough to get rid of him."

"What about turning him into the 'Ol Bill' wouldn't cost you a penny then." Claire offered,

"You know the rules we work by better than to ask me to 'grass' on one of our own." The suggestion had offended Big H because he had already committed that crime.

"The rules aint set in stone are they? And it would save you shelling out your own hard earned cash, it was only a suggestion."

Harry looked long and hard at the madam before leaving, "You can turn him in if you want, Claire, but my way rids us of him for good."

Big H walked out of the brothel one unhappy bloke.

Ray's car was taking him north again; he was travelling the length of the A1 all the way back to Scotland.

DCI Joe Brown was well pissed at two more corpses turning up on his patch; neither body had any ID, but the gun used was the same one as all the previous bodies.

"When's this gonna end? I need a connection between all these bodies and a lead on the culprit." Joe swallowed the whisky he'd poured himself, and, closing his eyes, he rubbed his forehead, "Jesus give me a fucking break, please."

"When you're asking for a favour from the big man himself Guv maybe you should leave out the swearing." The copper that had walked in to DCI Brown's office laughed at his own comment.

Joe looked up and glared at him. "Have you never heard of knocking?"

"Sorry Guv, but I thought you might like to hear this, the gun's the same for all the murders but it seems that the person responsible isn't, we have two different descriptions. The photofit from the B and B owner don't match the one from the café owner."

"Are we gonna get a break, some sort of a lead any time soon or just more complications?"

The copper walked out of the office after placing the photofit on the DCI's desk; the DCI poured himself another whisky. The man in charge of the murder cases, and hoping to solve them before he retired, sat at his desk and studied all the facts. There were a total of eleven bodies, and the killer they were after had committed all but one of them; he was one busy bastard, whoever he was. Four 'stiffs' had been found at Ron's gaff, two in a road close to where they worked, three in a bed and breakfast and two more on a different street, Ron's body was found before the other three making it five different murder scenes. "So what's the connection?" He asked himself, Joe Brown couldn't think of the answer, but he had a few clues. Ron and his missus were associates of Robert and the two corpses found with him, one gangster, three minders and one of their 'trouble and strife's'. A connection, however, to the other four bodies didn't seem to fit.

The two white-collar workers didn't fit in unless they were working for Robert and got hijacked by the trigger crazy killer, and the last two hadn't been identified, but their physiques said they could well have been 'heavies' too and if they were who were the muscle for? And then there was the prostitute; how was she connected?" The DCI's team had spoken to plenty of villains but came up with nada, zilch, nothing, so it was time for him to visit a few of them and apply a bit of pressure. Somebody out there knew something, and Joe Brown intended to find that person. The man lit up a fag and decided to visit Big H's office first. "He has to know more than he's told me up till now."

CHAPTER 31

"Those injuries look nasty Harry, did you trip down a flight of stairs or did the man I'm after give you a good hiding?"

DCI Joe Brown was sitting opposite Big H at his desk and was sure he saw the fat man flinch when he mentioned the beating, "I've just hit the nail right on its head haven't I Harry? So come on, give me something and I can put this man behind bars, that's where he belongs and if I don't catch him soon there aint gonna be any villains left on the streets and I'll be out of work." The DCI chuckled at his little joke; Big H didn't.

"Seriously Harry, this man needs taking off the street before he kills again and I think you can help me."

Big H remained silent; Joe stood up and walked around the desk and stood behind him. He placed a hand on each of Harry's shoulders and bent forward. "Give me something or I'm gonna start making life very difficult for you Harry. I'll have coppers in and out of here on a regular basis and following you when you go out. You'll find it very difficult to carry on with any business." The DCI returned to his seat and took out his packet of cigarettes; he lit up and inhaled and then blew the smoke straight at the villain. Big H didn't say or do anything, and so he repeated the operation. "Come on Harry give me something and I'll leave you alone."

Harry pulled open a drawer on his desk, and the DCI

jumped to his feet, but he didn't pull out a gun; he pulled out a photo instead and placed it on the desk. Joe picked it up and looked at it; it fitted one of his photofits back at the station. "And is he working alone? Cos this don't fit the first description we've got."

"Same bloke, he just altered his looks, I got the photo from Lizzie's boss, the madam at the brothel, apparently this bloke has been shagging one of the girls on a regular basis, and two of those bodies worked for her."

The DCI picked the photo up and left Big H's office; once outside, he allowed himself a satisfied grin before letting out a little laugh. "How the fuck did he get the name Big H?"

Big H wasn't happy with what he'd just done, snitching on one of his own, but he didn't need the aggro from the 'Old Bill' that the DCI had just promised. He also told himself that he could sleep better at night if the volatile nutter calling himself Ray was out of the way. The gangster poured himself a large whisky.

With most of her girls entertaining, Claire was not happy to have a top cop knocking at her door.

"It ain't a good time right now." She offered as an opening line.

"I don't suppose there is such a thing for you where I'm concerned but I ain't interested in any of your girls or what they're up to, just one of your clients." The DCI pushed past Claire and walked through to the living room; Claire followed him. He walked over to the drinks counter and lifted the stop out of one of the decanters; lifting it up to his nose, he sniffed, "Not the best", he commented but still poured a good measure into a glass for himself. "Care to join me?" Joe took the photo of Ray out of his jacket pocket and put it on the drinks cabinet, "I believe this bloke has been spending some time here, got the photo from Big H, I need to know where the murdering bastard is."

The DCI lifted the glass to his mouth and took a taste of the whisky he'd poured himself; pulling a face, he put the glass down and turned towards the madam. "Are you gonna help me or shall I have this place shut down?"

Claire smiled; the fact that Big H had been offended by her suggestion but had already committed the crime turned her smile into a laugh. The DCI started at the woman, "Are you gonna share the joke?"

"It's nothing, really."

Joe Brown shook his head and sighed. "Two more bodies have turned up and Big H tells me they were working for you, I need the connection between all of the corpses that have turned up so far so that I can put this murdering bastard calling himself Ray behind bars for the rest of his days."

Back in the operations room at the station DCI Brown allowed himself a smile. He had an audience and was looking forward to sharing his news with them.

"Listen up, you lot," their attention was not received, so Joe Brown banged his hand down hard on the table and repeated the order. Every one of them now had their eyes on him, and silence reigned in the room until the DCI broke it best part of a minute later. "Okay, I've been making myself busy and leaned on a couple of low-lifes and they have come up trumps for me."

Joe Brown had captured the attention of every single person in the room with his statement, and they were all eager to hear his news.

"I have a name," the DCI paused for effect before informing them all that it was 'Ray'. "No surname, and this could be an alias" the news received a few sighs of disappointment "but," there was another pause, "I have a photo."

DCI Brown lifted the photo he'd obtained from Big H and walked over to the notice board; he pinned the photo to it above the pictures of all the corpses and then turned back to face his audience. "This one man has killed all but one of the eleven bodies and I can now tell you that the eleventh body, Lizzie, was a prostitute who was there to take out Ray because he'd popped her brother who was working for the villain going by the name of Big H and his murder isn't included in that eleven." The other coppers shared a look before turning their attention back to Joe Brown.

"I don' know why he killed him but we have a name now so you can find out for me. It's all getting a bit messy but there are connections to all the murders and Big H and the brothel owner where Lizzie worked are both involved."

Joe Brown went on to tell his squad all that he knew before giving them Lizzie's brother's name, Robert.

A polite spattering of applause and several "Well done Guv" comments were uttered after the DCI had given up his info. A satisfied smile was returned to the audience before the DCI pulled a cigarette out of the packet that he took out of his jacket pocket and lit it up. He drew heavily on the tailor-made and inhaled deeply before blowing the smoke out.

"By the way, Guv", it was the same copper that had accompanied Joe to the east coast, "I know of this Robert and his partner Alan, if Robert's been taken out, then maybe Alan has too.

Joe Brown looked at the teller of more bad news and once again sighed with dismay, "When will this man stop killing, my guess is not before we have him in custody."

CHAPTER 32

The radio was on but Ray wasn't paying much attention, he was at the top end of the A1 and beyond renting a remote cottage with no phone or TV. When he wasn't listening to the radio, he was walking or sleeping. Life was remote and boring, but he knew he had to lay low for a while. After his last encounters with Claire and Big H, he guessed the price on his head had increased by a fair amount. The 'Old Bill' would also be keen on having a little chat with him, and he didn't want that. "How many life sentences, fucking hell, far too many years behind bars for my liking." He'd make do with his own company for a while longer.

CHAPTER 33

The two coppers sent to visit Kath, Lizzie and Robert's mum, were not looking forward to giving her the sad news about her two kids, even if she had given them up, she was still their mother and they guessed she must have feelings. When they met the wretched excuse for a mother they realised how wrong they had been. Her flat was a tip and she was a mess who, with empty beer cans and cheap cartons of wine on most of the flat's surfaces, obviously relied heavily on alcohol. The look they exchanged when the woman opened the front door and they walked into her property said how wrong they had been to have had those initial fears. Kath was wearing a slip and slippers, her make up had smudged, and her hair was unkempt. She had accepted the news with a shrug of the shoulders and a facial expression that showed surprise but lacked any feeling.

The two coppers left and were both relieved that Kath had not broken down and needed consoling, however her lack of emotion upset them both.

"Fuck me, not even so much as a tear from the heartless bitch."

The pair got back in their motor and drove back to the station.

Kath poured herself a glass of cheap wine from a carton and took it to bed with her.

Big H's physical damage to his body had managed to heal with time, but the embarrassment he felt from pissing his trousers twice in front of Ray had left a wound that could not be repaired so easily. Revenge was the only cure available for such an injury, but Ray had disappeared once again and, despite all of his efforts and that of his contacts he had not been able to find him.

"The little bastard 'll be back, I'll just have to be patient", but the anger he felt for Ray and his bladder weakness continued to peck away at him inside his head. "Fuck you Ray, I need you to suffer." Ray was invading his sleep too, Big H continued to have bad dreams, and the pistol-whipping plus the pissing of his pants was relived over and again in them, it was so real that when he woke with a start and shouting out his assailant's name in anger, he grabbed his crutch to make sure it was dry. He would then need to go to the bathroom and shower as a result of the sweating that accompanied each nightmare.

"The bastard has to pay for this," he told himself. The little fat man was becoming obsessed with the need for revenge, and as a result, his intake of whisky started to rise.

Claire's business was back to normal, the Old Bill were off her case, and the punters were back, but several of them missed the pleasures of a fuck with Lizzie, and Claire missed the income those fucks made for her. She, too, was angered by Ray's actions; he'd taken back his money, robbed her of the reward and left her tied up and naked for Big H to discover. Having had the holdall in her safe for such a short period of time pissed her off big time.

"It was a very large amount of money and more than made up for the loss of earnings I've suffered since he took out Lizzie. Fuck you Ray or whatever your name is, I really want that money back and I also need you to pay for what you've done." But her biggest grievance was with herself because of the orgasm she'd had when Ray had fucked her against her will; it topped how Big H had made her feel rubbing his podgy little hands over her as he'd untied her and helped her to her feet and the lecherous look he'd given while staring at her nakedness. When she added the loss of two of her minders to the list, Claire was one pissed off lady. "I really need you dead you bastard but I'd also like that holdall back." Claire poured herself a large vodka and topped it with a bit of orange juice, it would provide a bit of comfort, but the unease of what had happened was never far away from her thoughts, neither was the memory of being rescued by Big H. His look of pure lust at seeing her naked and tied had made her want to puke, but she'd needed him to untie her. When he did so, he then bent over and brushed against one of her tits with his hand and arm as he put them around her back and under her armpit. He'd pulled her up and his hand had rested on her other tit as he held her from behind to steady her with his stomach pushed against her arse. The memories made her finish her drink and then go to the cabinet to pour another.

"You dirty little perv!" She would need a third vodka and orange to erase the memories, albeit only for a short while; Claire shuddered after downing the second drink. She knew that it would be necessary to join forces with the grubby little bastard if she was ever going to exact any form of revenge against Ray. "Fuck only knows how many people he's bumped off and I don't wanna be added to that list." The madam made her way back to the cabinet for that third drink.

CHAPTER 34

Several months of solitude had passed for the hitman, and he was feeling the need for conversation with somebody other than himself. "Morning", "thank you", and "bye" had been the only words used whenever he'd bought groceries, and although tempted to call into the pub every time he passed it to get to the corner shop that he used, he'd managed to resist the temptation, buying a few tins of beer instead.

With no shaving or haircut since he'd left London, Ray was looking a bit unkempt but had no wish to visit a barbershop. "This'll do me just fine", he told himself as he observed his image in a mirror. He ran his fingers through the mass of hair atop his head and then used both hands to scratch his face through the beard. "It itches a bit but that's a small price to pay. Fuck, I don't even recognise myself." Ray laughed at his comment and then turned from the mirror and made his way to the fridge where he grabbed himself a can of beer; pulling the ring, he took a mouthful before making his way to the bedroom where he switched on the radio and then lay on top of the bed. "I'll give it a couple of more weeks and move south again I think". Ray took another swig of beer from the can and laughed at his suggestion. "Fuck me it's been too long without any fun."

Sat behind the wheel and heading south again, Ray still only had the radio for company, and so he sang along to the tunes he knew and held a conversation with the DJs in between the music. "You're going off your trolley son." Once again, Ray laughed at his comment.

It occurred to him that with the amount of money now in his possession, he could be driving a more luxurious motor. "I could be driving a Merc or a Jag, always fancied a Daimler Sovereign, think of the amount of petrol they'd drink though and, even though I can afford it, I don't think it's me. This money 'll come in handy when I retire."

Happy with his choice of motor, Ray continued with his journey south.

With the car parked, he booked himself into a bed and breakfast, "Just the one night for now thanks", he told the girl on reception; she passed him the room key and passed a pleasant smile in Ray's direction as he took it. Ray moved towards the staircase, and the girl concentrated on her book once more. He'd parted with his money and nothing else, signing the register with a false name. There had been no questions asked and no conversation; Ray was happy with that. Once inside the room, he put the holdall in the single wardrobe and looked around, a single bed, bedside cabinet with a lamp on and a chair made up the balance of contents in the room, not forgetting the small mat by the side of the bed. "I know how to spoil myself." Again Ray laughed at his comment and then made his way out of the room, locking the door behind him. Two minutes later, he was outside the B and B, taking in a large gulp of London air, with all the traffic back and forth it wasn't particularly fresh, and then exhaled. He decided to leave his motor where he had parked it and walked to a bus stop. One hour later, he was standing opposite the office of Big H, the short, rotund figure of the villain was standing staring out of the window with his hands in his trouser pockets, his trousers were held in place around his ample waist by a pair of braces. "Whoever gave him the name Big H must have had a good sense of humour." Every time Ray saw the villain, he had the same thought, and it always made him smile. Although the man was short in stature, he hadn't always been that round and had been a force to be reckoned with back in the day, handy with a flick knife he'd left his mark in the way of a 'mars bar' on many faces that fancied their chances in a 'bull and cow' with him. With the knife in his hand, Big H became six foot tall and cut many a man down in size. Since employing other thugs to do his dirty work Big H had been able to sit back on his laurels and allow his reputation to keep him safe and the money coming in. Robberies, protection, drugs and prostitution paid well and Big H had grown fat and unfit on the proceeds, but his workforce were a bunch of nasty bastards so it didn't matter, he paid well and they remained loyal to him.

Big H turned from the window and walked away; he was replaced by a six-foot block of muscle who looked over in Ray's direction and a minute later, the man walked out of the office with another bit of muscle that was just as big by his side. They looked left and right and waited for the traffic to ease before crossing the road. Ray felt uncomfortable seeing them and so while they waited on the pavement opposite he moved off at a pace. The pair crossed the road eventually, but the person they wanted was gone; looking all around, they shrugged their shoulders and made their way back to Big H, who was standing in the window once again with a less than happy look on his 'boat'.

"He's back, I know it, that was him, sure he looks different with all that hair and beard but I know that's him and I want him found."

Big H was feeling uncomfortable about what he had just seen, but with the two bodyguards with him twenty-four seven he felt safer than before. "Why is he back and what does the bastard want I wonder, I know what I want and that's him taken out."

A look of anger replaced the concerned one he'd been wearing as his mind once again raced back to the pistol-whipping he'd suffered and the humiliation of pissing himself not once but twice. "I need that little bastard to suffer while I watch." As the two lumps of muscle came back into the office, Harry looked at them both, "I know that was Ray and I want him found and brought to me."

"Yes boss." The two words were said in unison.

Big H sat himself down behind his desk and picked up his phone; the conversation he had was short, and he returned the receiver and prepared to wait for the return call. There was an unease about his composure that had his two minders looking at each other and shrugging. Big H noticed and barked at the pair of them. "He's one fucking dangerous bastard so don't treat him with contempt, his last spate of killings reached double figures and if he's back here he means to add to that total so show him the respect that his love for pulling the trigger deserves." Big H pulled his top draw open, "I need a fucking drink." After pouring a generous measure of whisky Big H looked up, "Do you both understand what I'm telling you?"

"Yes boss", a two-word answer that was said in unison once again. Big H sighed and took a mouthful of his drink.

When the figure entered the lobby, Claire looked up and smiled. "Hello Sir, first time here is it?" A warm smile followed the question, and the man returned the compliment with a "yes".

"Do you have any special requests? Hair colour, bust size, spanking or anything out of the ordinary, I have at least one girl here for most types of desires?" The warm smile was still in place.

"No, not really, just sex."

Claire stood up from behind the counter and moved off down a corridor; she looked at the customer and suggested he follow by beckoning him with her index finger. They passed three closed doors before finding one open. Claire walked in, and a petite but perfectly formed brunette girl stood up; she was wearing a see-through baby doll nightdress and nothing else except a smile, her tongue emerged from between her lips and caressed her top one and then she fluttered her eyelashes at her client, her big 'Bambi' eyes were bright and inviting. "Perfect", the man passed his money to Claire, who made her way out, closing the door behind her. Back behind her desk and minus the warm smile, Claire picked up her phone and returned the call that she had received earlier, "He's here and busy with one of my girls." Claire hung up and sat back. Big H's two goons left his office, promising to return with their prey. Claire needed a drink to calm her nerves; Big H took his bottle from the top drawer of his desk and poured himself another generous measure at the same time.

Ray wasn't too sure if Big H had recognised him or not, but when his muscle had made their way on to the street, he had decided to move on just in case. The fact that the madam hadn't seen through his new look reassured him, and he allowed the prostitute to remove his clothing and release his erection from the confinement of his underpants. His manhood was now being caressed by her tongue that she had teased him with earlier, and Ray was lost in the pleasure; he hadn't had any female attention all the time he'd been in Scotland, and he 'shot his load" far too quickly. The little brunette giggled at the ease with which she'd made her client climax and stood up. "Will it take long to make this chap stand up again?" she asked, caressing his bollocks at the same time. Ray, embarrassed by his premature ejaculation, pushed the girl away and started to dress. "I'll call again tomorrow", he muttered and, once he was dressed, he left her room. His early emergence took Claire by surprise, and she almost choked on her drink; the coughing fit that followed had Ray less than pleased, and he walked straight past her and out of the brothel.

Several expletives escaped from her lips in between her coughs, and, flustered, Claire picked up the phone and dialled Big H.

Ray exited the drive to the brothel just as a car carrying Harry's muscle pulled in.

"Bollocks, he had recognised me and so had that bitch." Ray pushed his accelerator hard to the floor and sped off; the muscle had recognised him too and carried out a three-point turn in a manner that would have had them fail a driving test, but by the time they reached the road Ray and his car were out of sight. The pair were big, and both could handle themselves, but neither of them was looking forward to their next encounter with their boss. "Bollocks" escaped their lips, and it was in unison once again. The return journey was made in silence.

Ray returned to his B and B and collected his belongings; his escape had been too close for his liking and, although he'd had an adrenaline fix, he'd decided to have it on his toes and head north again.

It was time to rethink his future. There would be no form of retribution carried out for the gangster or the madam; Harry and Claire's nightmares would continue for the time being.

CHAPTER 35

Knowing that it wasn't in his nature to become a hermit, he didn't want to become a socialite either; Ray knew he couldn't live as remote as he had been for the last couple of months. The holdall he carried about with him also guaranteed that he didn't need to work for a long time, but his love for violence and the buzz he received from inflicting pain on others (it was an even bigger fix when he put a bullet in their head) said he couldn't stay unemployed for too long. Ray put a few miles between himself and London; he'd passed Oxford and Stratford-upon-Avon and arrived in Manchester, booking in to another B & B for the night. Leaving his holdall in the wardrobe once more, the man left in pursuit of a beer, a bit of grub and some serious thinking. Five minutes later he'd parked his arse on a seat in a boozer where he hoped he would achieve his goals, the need for a beer and a meal was easily satisfied, but as the place got busier any serious thinking would have to be put on hold. The jukebox and the buzzing sound of conversation interjected with laughter, and the occasional shriek of an excited female filled the air; Ray got himself another beer and sat back and relaxed as best he could. He was a new face and knew nobody here knew him, but he felt the need to keep his wits about him just in case anything untoward happened; it was an occupational hazard. He had learned to live with his guard up, he'd made a big mistake when he allowed himself to have feelings for Brenda, and that one big error was the reason he was here now, she appeared in his head and smiled at him, Ray sighed at the vision and half smiled before pulling himself upright in the chair and lifting his beer off the table.

"Leave the past in the past for fuck's sake, Ray," he told himself and returned to the present. He finished his beer and decided to have one more before heading off and leaving the crowd to enjoy their evening without him. He waited his turn at a busy bar and ordered a pint of bitter.

The barmaid smiled at him, "Not from around here are you? Accent says you're from further south."

Ray returned the smile but did not reply.

"Silent, moody type eh?" The barmaid laughed at her comment; Ray continued to smile and proffered the money in exchange for his pint. "Do you not like what you see man? I'm trying to make conversation here you ignorant bastard." The barmaid, a blonde-haired little bombshell with an hourglass figure and good looks, pouted at Ray; she wasn't used to being ignored and put the pint of bitter down heavily on the bar.

"Just out for a quiet beer, sorry", Ray offered in the way of an apology and, picking his pint up, he turned to walk away, but his exit was blocked by a geezer who obviously spent a fair bit of time visiting the gym.

"We don't like your type coming up here and thinking you're better than us."

Ray looked the muscle-bound brute in front of him straight in the eye, looking up to do so. "I said sorry and I'm after drinking this beer and leaving." Ray kept eye contact the whole time.

"Are you trying to stare me out, or maybe you're trying to intimidate me like." Muscles looked around to see if he had an audience; it wasn't much of one, so he pushed Ray in the chest and raised his voice, "You Londoners are all the same, flash bastards who think you're better than us", a second push followed the comment and Ray had to cede ground under the force, the audience had grown, Ray turned to the bar and put his pint down, the barmaid was smiling now that she had her knight in shining armour defending her, Ray slipped his right hand into his pocket and slid the set of knuckle dusters on as he returned the smile before turning around and smashing a right-hander straight into the beefcake's 'kisser', moving forward he grabbed the geezer by his shoulders and pulled him forward and down lifting his knee at the same time, it collided with the bloke's bollocks, and he let out a grunt of displeasure. A second right-hander smashed into the side of the head, blood was pouring from the bloke's nose and mouth as a result of the first blow and skin broke under the force of the second; as he crashed to the floor, most of the audience, now considerably bigger, gasped in disbelief at what they'd just witnessed, "Fuckin' 'ell, did you see that eh?"

"I fuckin' did," said another bloke who rushed at Ray. "You southern bastard."

Ray timed his punch to perfection, and his assailant went crashing to the floor. "Fuckin' 'ell he's done it again", the person with the squeaky little voice started to clap and giggle with delight, "Who's next eh? Anybody else fancy their fuckin' chances?" Ray looked over to where the voice was coming from; it belonged to a little man who hadn't been at the front of the queue when the good looks had been handed out; he watched as another bloke slapped the pipsqueak across the back of his head. "Shut the fuck up you twat", the little man fell forward, and the attacker pushed past him and straight towards Ray, another direct hit from his right hand spread victim number 3. Ray now moved with speed towards the door, and his audience parted Red Sea style as he made his exit. Once outside, Ray took a quick look behind to see if he was being followed before setting off at a brisk pace; he slipped his 'duster' back in his pocket.

"I guess I've outstayed my welcome here as well," he glanced over his shoulder; nobody was following, so he slowed his pace to normal and made his way back to the B and B. The following morning saw him setting off further north towards Kendal. He pulled into a roadside café after half an hour of driving and had breakfast. It was after the early rush and before the customers started to arrive for their lunch so fairly quiet, and the woman serving was middle-aged, overweight and wearing a skirt that finished mid-calf with no shape to it, a thick jumper that seemed to be struggling to contain the rolls of flesh below and a pair of boot style slippers. She wasn't interested in conversation, and that suited Ray. He paid for the fry up and put the change in her tip jar; the woman nodded in appreciation and then set about cooking; Ray took a seat facing the door and waited. Twenty minutes later, he was back behind the wheel of his car.

Big H was less than pleased with his two hired muscle standing in front of him; they both stared at the floor while he gave them a bollocking and then sent them packing. "I won't need your help now, the bastard won't be coming back here fore a while, you fucked up big time, what did you do, take the fuckin' scenic route there?"

Big H handed them some money, and the pair left his office without reply.

Claire was not happy with her worker, either.

"What the fuck happened, you were supposed to keep him entertained for longer than a few minutes, did he not fancy ya?"

The girl smiled at her boss, "The exact opposite actually, I started to play with him and it was all over, easiest money I've made in a long while, anyway I think he was embarrassed by the early ending and copped a strop."

Claire shook her head. "That was the bastard that tied us all up and killed the two minders a couple of months back, he robbed the safe too which is something that he needed to pay for but it never happened because you didn't do your job properly."

Claire's voice rose higher as she spoke, and the girl adopted a sad face and mumbled her apology before walking away.

Claire made her way to the drinks cabinet. "I should have let him fuck me again, he'd have been dealt with if I had, now we have to wait until he comes back again and in the meantime there he is inside my head tormenting me." Claire swallowed the vodka and orange in one go and poured herself another one, "Bollocks."

CHAPTER 36

Ray passed through Kendal and its grey limestone buildings and continued the journey toward Glasgow, it was another 142 miles of driving, and the radio helped soften the boredom. Four miles out of Glasgow was a place called Bishop Briggs, and that's where Ray planned to stay for a while. It was middle-classed and with a population of around 23000 would prove ideal for his wants, not too remote but not too busy either and with a short commute to Scotland's largest city where Ray hoped to find work. Gang warfare and crime were prolific on the east side of Glasgow, and the hitman was sure he'd be able to find work there with over forty rival gangs in that part of the city. He wouldn't be going anywhere without his gun or knuckle dusters, though.

After booking into a guest house, Ray took a walk around the shopping centre and then called into a pub for a drink and some food; it wasn't late when he'd finished eating, so he decided to have an afternoon nap before heading into Glasgow. This meal had passed without incident, and so a grateful Ray returned to the guest house and took the siesta he'd promised himself; he'd covered a fair few miles and needed to be fresh before going out that evening.

Showered and dressed, Ray put some money in his pocket, not enough to be mugged for and not in a wallet that might draw attention, drinking would be kept to a minimum as he needed to keep his wits about him, a pair of eyes in the back of his head would be a useful addition, but he wasn't going to get them any time soon so he'd have to rely on his wits.

It was only a short walk from the guest house to Glasgow city centre, and it did not take long before Ray found himself on the east side that boasted a cathedral and the Necropolis, a Victorian garden cemetery that showed views of Glasgow, it was also home to an outside museum and art gallery. Ray passed them all with little interest and headed further east towards Dennison, an area famous for its eateries, especially Italian cuisine; none of this was of any interest to Ray either, he was hoping to come across the darker side of the area, and a short walk past the restaurants took him to where he wanted to be. There were gangs of youths on the corners of all turnings smoking and drinking, and the whiff of joints filled the air as he passed each gathering; Ray also noticed bottles of whisky being passed around and guessed most of these gang members came from families that lived on the bread line, poverty ruled here, and so the crime rate would be high. As Ray passed each group of youths, he kept his hands in his pockets; one hand caressed his gun and the other his knuckle dusters. He got the odd look from one or two of the youngsters but was mostly ignored.

"What am I doing here and what do I hope to find?" Ray was questioning his sanity, "If I open my mouth my accent is gonna land me in deep shit so I don't think I'm gonna find any work here." Feeling stupid, Ray decided to head back to the restaurants where he felt more comfortable, but his return trip was noticed by one gang member who stepped out in front of him and held his arm out to stop Ray passing.

"What you doin' here wee man, you should nae be

walking up and down these streets, they're a wee bit dangerous." The statement drew the attention of the other gang members, and they formed a ring around the intruder; Ray tried to walk on but had an outstretched hand push firmly against his chest, "have you got a tongue wee man? I asked what you were doin' here so I did."

"I was…" only two words passed Ray's lips before he was pushed backwards and then forward, then sideways.

"What 'ave we got ourselves here then, a wee Sassenach?" The comment drew laughs, and Ray suddenly felt vulnerable.

"The boots on the other fuckin' foot now", he thought, "and I can't get my back against a wall."

Ray needed to think fast, he was still being shoved from side to side, and the shoves were getting harder and faster as the laughs grew louder; he wasn't used to being the underdog and did not know how to escape the situation.

"Hey wee man, you did nae tell us why you're here."

Ray pulled out his gun and fired a shot in the air; everybody jumped back and turning 360 degrees; Ray pushed through the ring and, pointing the gun at the gang, started walking backwards, "I'm in the wrong place but I'm leaving now, sorry." Ray kept on taking steps backwards, nobody moved or spoke, and he was feeling more comfortable with each step that he made; he turned his head for a quick glance behind, and as he did, he walked into a lamppost and lost his balance, the gang roared with laughter and ran at Ray who tried to steady himself, but the distance he'd covered wasn't enough, and soon he was on the floor with bodies on him, they were kicking and punching, and Ray lost grip of the gun under the onslaught. The attack was vicious, and the hitman heard himself crying out in pain until he arrived at a darkness that was filled with peace, and although he was still being used as a football come punch bag, the pain had finally stopped for him.

CHAPTER 37

Squinting through the slits where his 'minces' were Ray didn't recognise his surroundings, his vision was somewhat limited because he couldn't open them properly; realising he was horizontal, he tried to sit up but yelled out in pain under the attempt and collapsed back to the floor. Ray didn't know where he was or why he was there, but the pain and lack of vision told him he was in deep shit.

He must have lost consciousness again, for how long Ray didn't know, but he was awoken by a gentle nudging of his shoulder; he could hear a voice talking softly to him. The poor battered bastard tried to sit up, but pain reached every part of his bruised body, and he cried out in pain under the effort and collapsed yet again.

"You stay there Sonny, I'll away and get some help, a few wee minutes, no more."

Ray laughed at the comment, "I'd love to get up and have it away on me toes, lady, but that aint gonna happen so I guess I'll still be here when you get back."

"Jack willl sit with you, you'll be okay with him by your side."

Ray was just about to ask who Jack was when a big wet tongue wiped his face; this action was followed by a deep booming bark.

"I don't know what type of dog you are Jack, but you sound like a big bastard."

Jack let out another bark, and then there was silence for what seemed like an eternity to Ray; it was a pain-filled wait and he made no attempt to move again until his saviour returned with the help that she'd promised.

"Now I'm guessing ya do nae want the police or an ambulance so my two wee brothers here are gonna lift you into this 'ere chair and push you to my wee house so I can clean ya up a wee bit. Okay boys, grab him under his arms and lift him and do nae hang around 'cos it's gonna hurt anyway so better short and sharp so it is."

Ray had no time to prepare for the onslaught of pain that was about to happen and wouldn't have known how to anyway; the torture filled agony that suddenly surrounded and encompassed his body was full of glittering stars, and then a kaleidoscope of pain-filled patterns were swirling around in his 'nut'. He yelled out at his suffering, hideous, distressed sounds exited from his lips, and suddenly he was sitting in a wheelchair and being pushed along. Every small discretion that the chair found in the pavement had Ray parting with another involuntary pain-filled shriek but whoever his saviours were, they seemed oblivious to the agony that they were inflicting on him. The pushing finally slowed, and then he was being pulled in reverse up steps; he didn't count how many but wailed in pain with each one. The steps were followed by a short pull in reverse and then a push forward before the wheelchair came to a halt, and Ray felt hands grab hold under each arm, lift him and then spin him 180 degrees before sitting him in another chair. The pain-filled shrieks had turned into whimpers now, Ray could no longer find the energy to scream, and then the journey to where ever he'd been taken was over and the relief that filled him burst out of his pores, he found himself laughing until his head fell forward and blackness enveloped his being once more.

Ray's 'minces' opened but not very wide; however, it

was wide enough to see where he was, and he saw his surroundings for the first time; humble was the word he would use to describe them, but his gratitude for the help he'd received was overflowing. As he looked around, he suddenly focused on a woman, red hair draped over her shoulders and her figure along with her good looks made for a nice view, Ray smiled, and the figure returned the compliment; she was the first to speak and told Ray he'd been in the chair for five days, Ray was shocked by the news and then listened to her tell him where she had found him, he tried to thank her, but she told him to be quiet and went on to explain that his rent money, food and nursing costs were due. The figure she gave Ray caused him to splutter and then laugh. "It's nae joke wee man." The smile had left the woman's face, and she pointed out that if he didn't pay, she would hand him back to the gang that had inflicted all those painful injuries on him and were the culprits for all the misery he was being subjected to at this present time.

"Who should I make the cheque out to?" he asked; his attitude did not impress his saviour who scowled at him, the redhead left the room, and when she returned a few minutes later, she had company in the form of two hairy-arsed gorillas, there was one either side of her, Jack followed them into the room, he was an impressive looking rottweiler who let out a deep bark when he saw Ray. "These two wee un's are my brothers and helped getting you here where you've been safe, they will nae hesitate to take you back where we found you if I ask them. You have nae money or anything with you so the wee bastards mugged ya but I'm certain you have means by which you can settle your wee debt." The woman passed a smile in Ray's direction that told him she was holding all the cards, "And Jack here has nae been fed yet." On cue, the dog barked again, and Ray swallowed hard; he was trying to remember how he'd got to be in this mess and why he was stuck with the bird, her two gorillas and Jack, he'd guessed he was in Scotland but wasn't sure why he was there.

"You can stay her a while more so you can, but the cost will be more. My two wee boys along with Jack will look after you until you're ready to leave."

The two gorillas moved over to Ray and placed a hand on each of his shoulders, and leaned forward. "You d'nae wanna be messing with us big man, a wee Sassenach turning up dead won't raise much interest here and nae body's come looking for ye so we reckon you're on your own."

Some pressure was applied to each shoulder that caused Ray considerable discomfort before the two goons left the room, leaving their dog behind; Jack sat opposite Ray and stared at him, which was unsettling, to say the least. The redhead moved forward; she was wearing skin-tight jeans that clung tightly to her arse, and the short-sleeved V neck jumper was struggling to contain her tits, the woman leaned forward just like the two blokes had, but the view was so much better.

"Under different circumstances…" Ray thought, his eyes stuck to the cleavage like glue.

"It would nae ever happen Sonny, you get some rest now and we'll talk some more later."

The redhead stood up, and placing a hand on either side of her breasts, gave them a squeeze. Ray's 'minces' nearly popped out of his head. The woman laughed and left the room; Jack did not move. It was time for the hitman to start remembering and figure a way out of this mess.

Two more days passed, and, true to her words, his saviour kept him fed and watered. With a considerable effort, Ray managed to pull himself upright into a standing position and tell her he needed a piss.

"You take yourself this time; it'll be the first time in a week."

Ray didn't want to ask who had taken him before but

guessed it was the two gorillas. Ray's memory had returned, and he knew he could pay the debt, but the rates were extortionate, and he didn't want to. He was pretty sure he was in possession of a gun and a set of 'dusters' which would even the odds a bit when he came to pay. Remembering where his B and B was, Ray went to collect his belongings and the holdall stuffed with cash; the redhead's two brothers accompanied him. Ray paid for his room with money that he took out of the bag and was gutted to find that his gun and dusters were not there. He then remembered taking them with him. "The bastards have 'half-inched' them along with the money I had on me". Thankfully the keys to his car were on the table by the bed beside his wallet; as he went to pick them up, he was knocked sideways, "We'll be having them until you pay your dues, Sonny,"

Ray was in no position to argue, so one of his new mates drove his motor for him.

Back at his temporary accommodation Ray was escorted back to the living room; the redhead was waiting for him with Jack, and Ray was somewhat surprised when she told her two brothers to leave the room, he was even more shocked when she told him to strip bullock naked but, in anticipation of a fuck, he did as he was told. Walking over to him, the redhead, who had never told Ray her name, smiled and grabbed his cock, it responded, and she released a little giggle that Ray found sexy; she then pushed her tongue out and ran it slowly over her top lip. Ray's cock was now throbbing with anticipation, but then she squeezed it so hard he thought it was going to explode, Ray cried out in pain, and she released her grip; a large sigh of relief escaped Ray's lips, but then his tormentor squeezed again. The hitman wanted to punch the bitch's lights out, but then he'd have to get past the rottweiler and then wrestle her two goons to get his car keys; he was in too much pain still from his kicking to engage in any serious combat, so he whimpered as the pain increased and then the grip was released, Ray sighed again, and his tormentor laughed as she squeezed once more before letting go and picking up his clothes.

"I'm gonna give these wee clothes a wash for ye and then you can pay your bill, I'll give ye back your clothes and you can be on your way." The redhead looked down at his cock once more and caressed her lip with her tongue, there was no response from Ray's now limp dick, and the woman laughed as she left the room with Jack close behind and then Ray was alone in the room, naked and cold.

As much as it hurt him, Ray knew he would be paying the monies due in full. After he'd healed, he would maybe return and take the cash back. For the time being, though, he sorted the cash and a couple of hours later, he exchanged it for his clean clothes and car keys.

"Fuck Scotland", he told himself "I'm heading south again, I just made a big and expensive mistake coming here."

CHAPTER 38

It took the hitman longer than he had hoped to make a full recovery from the kicking he had received, but he got there; he just needed to join a gym now and get back to a level of fitness that would allow him to return to work. He had been staying in a small town in Hertfordshire where nobody knew him, and he'd managed to keep his nose clean for the entire time he'd been there, he'd made London and all his previous haunts a 'no-go' area but would return when he was ready, have a little nose around and see what was going on, he'd purchase a new gun and dusters first though.

Time passed, and Ray's fitness returned, armed with his new tools of the trade, he decided to head back to Scotland and settle a few scores, the kicking and being ripped off didn't sit easy with the hitman; he would feel so much better after meting out a violent punishment to both parties and this time, with a plan in the place he would be in total control of both situations.

The gang had inflicted more pain on Ray than he wanted to remember, but the beating had haunted his sleep on so many occasions and always resulted in him waking up dressed in a cold sweat and raging at his tormentors with an outburst of violent abuse so he would deal with them first. The plan was simple, he would return to the corner where they hung out, but this time in his car, let his car window down and call out for their attention and then, as they approached, open fire before driving away.

"Oi you scabby arsed jocks" got their attention, the gang looked at each other, nodded and then began their approach; Ray lifted his gun and pulled the trigger six times, every bullet claimed a life and happy with his work, the assassin drove off looking in his rearview mirror as he did so. He saw a couple of gang members chasing after him and so stopped the car and allowed them to catch up. One of them raised his arm and took aim; Ray guessed that it was probably the gun they'd nicked off him; he put the car in reverse and sped at them, he knocked them both down and drove over their bodies before changing to first gear and accelerating the car towards them, running over them for a second time, tightly holding onto the steering wheel he managed to keep control of his car, and then he sped off looking in his rearview mirror for a second time, neither body was moving. A loud "Yes" left his lips followed by a laugh, he was aware that the next helping of retribution he was about to dish out could prove to be a tad more difficult, but he was riding on a high now and convinced he would get the job done with speed and efficiency. First, though, he needed a different set of wheels, the redhead and her two brothers knew this car, and it may also have been seen by any witnesses there might have been to the shootings he'd just carried out. Ray stopped at a petrol station and bought a can that he filled with a gallon of petrol; he also filled the tank of the car with fuel before finding a quiet spot and dowsing the car with the gallon of petrol he set it ablaze. A steady half-hour walk brought him back to civilisation, where he found a café and grabbed a bite to eat. Ray waited until nightfall before catching a bus to Glasgow. His return to Bishop Briggs was made in a car he'd 'half inched', breaking into it and then hotwiring the ignition. He parked up near the redhead's gaff and had a gander in its direction; the living room lights were on, but no curtains drawn. He could see the 'bonces' of the two goons above the sofa they were sitting on; they were busy watching TV. Ten minutes later their sister came into the room with two plates of sandwiches and handed them to the pair; the redhead then left the room. Ray stepped out of his motor and walked over to the window; he took his gun out of his pocket and fitted the silencer; he was wearing gloves and carrying a hammer in his left hand. Breaking the glass, Ray popped a bullet in the back of each of their heads before they managed to move; Jack stood up and made to leap at Ray, he buried a bullet in the dog's head before he moved to the front door and waited, but not for too long, the redhead opened the door and made to run out on to the pavement, Ray's shove that he gave her sent her back in the direction from which she'd just come, and he followed her into the house and closed the door behind him. The redhead landed in an unceremonious heap halfway down the passage, and Ray was on her before she could regain her composure.

"Get up bitch."

She looked up and saw who her assailant was, there was a look of disbelief on her kisser and then she shouted for her boys, but they never came, "Open the door" Ray barked the order at the woman and, looking first at him and then the gun, she did as she was told, the site that met her caused her to scream out in anger and turn towards their killer.

"Ya…" the bullet tore through her forehead and exited through the back of her head, causing the redhead to fall backwards and land on top of her brothers; Ray turned and walked out, a 'Cheshire cat' grin stretched across his kisser.

On his way back to Hertfordshire, Ray dumped the stolen motor in Bedfordshire and then made his way home on public transport. Home, for now, was still the rented flat, and once inside, he lay back on the settee feeling happy with his work even though it had been a long day. Ray had added another eleven bodies to the ever-growing list of corpses; he soon nodded off but was never alone in his sleep and once again woke with a start, there was always somebody exacting a grizzly revenge, and he was always helpless, unable to stop them. They were ghosts from his ugly past, but it was the path he'd chosen to walk, and these bad dreams, unfortunately, walked alongside him. Ray took a shower and then made himself a cup of coffee. "What next my son?" he asked himself the question but didn't provide the answer, a large sigh exited from his body, and he was given another glimpse of the dream that had caused him to wake up; his body shuddered in response, Ray used his left hand to administer two slaps to his 'boat race.'

"Get a grip for fuck's sake son!"

Ray took notice of his own advice and finished his coffee before readying himself for a run. After that, he would return to the gym he'd joined; he felt he needed to keep up his fitness level before entering the lion's den once more. His actions must have left both Big H and Claire hungry for revenge, and wounded lions were dangerous animals.

Ray let several more weeks pass, every day following the same routine, a run in the morning, the gym, where he pumped iron every afternoon and an early evening walk that was followed by dinner then some TV before bed, every night Ray's sleep continued to bring him the uninvited visitors that caused him to wake with a start.

He'd seen the mess that he'd left in Scotland on the national news. The carnage caused and number of deaths had the police baffled, and because the two attacks had been committed on the same night, the 'Old Bill' were busy trying to find something that would link them, but that was proving difficult.

Ray knew, however, that he'd just added a whole new load of visitors into his head, and they would all be there in his bad dreams every night carrying out their own forms of retribution; interrupted sleeps were a certainty for the foreseeable future at the very least.

Having kept his head down for a few weeks and now feeling the benefits of his running and weights, Ray decided it was time to look for some paid work again. He'd been living the life of a monk for those few weeks, staying in Hertfordshire and, apart from the odd exchange of a nod with a few neighbours and, just like his stay in rural Scotland, a greeting of normally just one word 'Hello', 'Morning' or 'Afternoon' and a 'Thank you' in the shops, he'd only had chats with himself, the funny thing was he wasn't bored by the conversations.

Venturing back into London and meeting either Claire or Big H was suicidal but exciting too, and a face to face with either of them aroused Ray. "But I need a woman first," he told himself, and that evening he knocked watching the tele on the head and went out to find one. "A no strings attached fuck is what I need, so it has to be a visit to a brothel."

CHAPTER 39

Having satisfied his needs, Ray's thoughts were now with Brenda. He was questioning his own sensibility for developing feelings but wondered if he would have given everything up for her and settled down to enjoy the 'happy ever after' life they had planned. "I doubt it," he told himself, "you'd miss the buzz you get every time you inflict pain or death." He knew he was right, and that's what he told himself before allowing his thoughts to leave Brenda in the past and move on to Big H and Claire. Ray knew the pair were as thick as thieves, and so a visit to either would result in a phone call being made. He didn't need Claire; there were other brothels, but the thought of paying her a visit and bringing all those bad memories back into her head excited him, and he wouldn't mind fucking her again but guessed she wouldn't give that freely. "Maybe I'll give her a visit just for the hell of it." Ray laughed at his thought, and when he remembered the sex, he felt a little bit of movement in his underpants; Ray squeezed his crutch through his trousers and then turned his thoughts to Big H. He was sure that, despite all the pain and embarrassment he'd inflicted on the villain, he would receive a warm welcome and the offer of work. "It would give the little fat man the opportunity of setting me up again and fulfilling his need for revenge."

Ray sat back on the sofa and afforded himself a smile.

"It could be exciting playing with danger, risking everything again just to hurt him some more when he fails."

Ray was certain of his next move now; the only question left to answer, was when he needed more time at the gym, he guessed he'd have to be at the top of his game to win this final battle. Another laugh exited his lips, "See you soon, Harry, very soon."

Everything had been very quiet for Joe Brown, the number of corpses had not risen, but there had been no more leads either, and Big H and Claire hadn't offered any more information despite the additional pressure he had put on both of them, he knew the name of the killer but not his whereabouts, It looked like his imminent retirement would arrive before he could solve the multiple cases. He guessed that he wouldn't be leaving the force in a blaze of glory but then if he had solved the case and brought the killer to justice, would it have given him a bigger pension? No was the answer to that question, and so Joe Brown was fairly happy to leave the job of solving the murders in the hands of his successor.

With London so close, Ray decided to put off buying another car for the moment and commute. It was cold enough outside to wear a coat, and that would help him conceal his gun and knuckle dusters without drawing any attention to himself.

"You've got some nerve coming back here after your last visit." The look of surprise on the face of Big H when Ray had walked into his office was obvious, as was the want to pull out his gun and shoot the bastard dead. Once again, Big H's attempt to hide his thoughts had failed.

Ray smiled. "Hello Harry, good to see you again."

A blank, expressionless look returned to Big H's face, but Ray could see the nervousness there; Big H was frightened of him, and that fear was a possible danger for Ray, something he was aware of, and it excited him.

"I need work and money, Harry, so let's forget the past and look to the future. I've always made you money so let's get back to that."

Ray proffered his hand in Big H's direction, which caused him to flinch, the pain he'd received from the bastard was there again in front of everything else including, for a split second, reason, and Harry could feel it, but he resisted the urge to scream and go for his gun; instead, he took a deep breath and exhaled slowly. Ray watched closely and was inside the villain's head with his thoughts.

"Put them thoughts out of your head, Harry, and let's do business, one job that's all and we both make money and move on, either of us dying won't do the other one any favours."

Big H continued to resist the need to scream at Ray and fight back the monstrous urge to reach for his gun; he took another deep breath and exhaled slowly again, the urges slowly ebbed away, and Big H forced a smile, "You're right, Ray, we were good together so one more job sounds good to me." Big H stood up and accepted Ray's offer of a handshake. "Call back here tomorrow and I'll have a package put together for you."

Ray let go of Harry's hand and returned the smile. "You get that package together, Harry, and I'll ring with a place to meet, somewhere public so neither of us does anything silly."

Ray walked backwards to the door and opened it, "See you tomorrow Harry."

Ray left, and Big H waited a minute before he released the scream he'd kept suppressed throughout the visit; he stood up and slammed his right fist down heavily on the top of the desk, "You're dead you bastard, fucking dead." Big H opened his desk drawer and took out the bottle of scotch and glass; after pouring and then swallowing a large measure, he picked up his phone and called Claire. Half an hour later, they were sitting opposite each other, deep in conversation. They toasted their plans with a large whisky each that Big H poured, and then Claire left. Her thoughts were back to Ray raping her and the anger she had felt when she'd orgasmed, but time had managed to ease that feeling. "I wouldn't say no to a second fuck from the bastard," the thought excited her, and she couldn't remove it from her head "you're fuckin' with my nut Ray and I don't like it but after tomorrow you'll be gone."

Claire got into her motor and closed her eyes, but Ray invaded her darkness too, he was there fucking her, and she was enjoying it all the way to the orgasm. She opened her eyes and looked down at her crutch, she realised she had been rubbing herself with the palm of her hand, and as she lifted it away, she revealed a damp patch on her trousers. "I fuckin' hate you, you bastard" Claire started to bash the steering wheel with her fists and screamed. It wasn't the first time that this had happened, but it was the angriest she had felt afterwards. How could she relive a rape, and it had that effect, it was an indecent pleasure that she hated herself for having.

Claire cuffed away the tears with the sleeve of her jacket before starting up the engine and driving off. Harry watched her drive away; his thoughts were now about her, and the vision of her lying naked and bound on the floor excited him; Big H made his way to the bathroom and turned on the shower, stripping naked he took hold of his cock and under the running water he relieved himself with the image of a naked Claire staying with him throughout.

CHAPTER 40

Returning back to Hertfordshire, Ray was more than happy with the day's work. "I'll bet Big H has been in touch with Claire and the pair of them are planning their revenge." Ray laughed, "it could be just like a movie tomorrow when we meet, but if it turns into a gunfight I'll have to be quick on the draw!" Ray realised that the odds were against him but didn't mind being the underdog; after all he was choosing when and where they would meet. The hit man opted to eat out and then retired to his bed early, he needed to be on the ball the following day.

Morning arrived after another night of restless sleep and Ray showered and shaved before putting on a white shirt and black suit. Standing in front of a full length mirror in the bedroom, he took a good look at himself. "You're a handsome bastard, Ray." The man then laughed and, after putting his 'dusters' in the right-hand jacket pocket and pistol in the inside pocket, he left his apartment. He would arrive in London before calling Big H and limit the time the gangster would have to organise anything. This was going to be a big day for Ray and maybe, just maybe, his last but he walked with a confident bounce in his step, he knew there would be no work on offer just an end to their relationship and one of their lives.

Ray arrived in London and chose a bar on a busy street

as his choice of a meeting place. He then informed Harry of his whereabouts and gave him fifteen minutes to make it there. "Plenty of time Big H, and come alone with the work offer." Ray allowed himself a smile as he hung up knowing that Harry didn't have much time to arrange a back-up, however he had plenty of time to slip a gun into his jacket pocket. If Harry had rung Claire she was thirty minutes away, it would all be over before she arrived, and if he brought a couple of heavies with him he'd be dropping them off and they would have to finish the journey off on 'shanks's pony'. It left Ray a small window of opportunity, about five minutes maximum by his reckoning, to remove the threat of revenge that he knew 'Big H' so wanted. The fact that he'd waited this long since his last failed attempt was obviously due to the fact that Ray had disappeared but now he was back on the scene and Big H would be looking forward to this meeting as much as Ray was but probably pissed off that he wasn't calling the shots.

Ray positioned himself at the far end of the bar and although there was plenty of foot traffic on the street the pub itself wasn't as busy as he'd have liked but it would have to do. He sat on a bar stool facing the door and kept patting his pocket to make sure his gun was still there. "Of course it's still there; get a grip for fucks sake!" The reprimand he'd just given himself didn't stop him patting the pocket again just a minute later.

The door to the bar opened and a single bloke walked in and walked to the counter where he ordered a pint, the barman made no attempt at conversation with the customer. "Not a regular." Ray decided to keep an eye on him. A quick look at his watch told him Big H would be arriving in the next two minutes; Ray patted his jacket pocket again and looked at the last customer to enter the bar. The bloke was staring in his direction and as Ray made eye contact he quickly turned away, too quickly for Ray's liking. "He's one of Big H's men for sure." The door opened again and this time it was Harry who walked into the bar, Ray raised his arm and caught his attention, Big H waved back and made his way over, Ray was sure the villain gave a slight nod of the head as he passed the other newcomer, and then he was standing in front of him, neither of them offered their hand for a shake and both seemed on edge. Ray rose his hand and stuck his index finger up to get the barman's attention "Two single malts when you're ready." The barman acknowledged the request and collected two glasses. As he poured the drink, Ray put his hand in his pocket and took out his wallet, it caused Big H to put his hand in his pocket too and when he saw Ray take out his wallet his face reddened. Ray smiled "I'll get these Harry, have you brought a contract of work with you?"

"Of course Ray, all the details are on this piece of paper."

Ray took out a bank note from his wallet and put it on the counter in exchange for the two single malts, he'd been distracted and in that moment Big H had his pistol in his hand and pointing at Ray, the barman saw the gun and let out a low moan before walking away hurriedly. Ray kicked up at the stool Big H was sat on and toppled it backwards, Harry pulled the trigger and the bullet left the gun as he fell in a backward motion toward the floor and buried itself in the pub's ceiling. The gangster landed with a thud but kept hold of his gun, however, he couldn't regain his composure in time and Ray buried a bullet in his chest. He then looked up to see Harry's sidekick coming towards him, gun in hand. Ray squeezed the trigger for a second time and the geezer stopped dead in his tracks and then fell forward. There was panic in the bar now with customers screaming and running for the door, pushing each other out of the way in their flee for safety, the barman had crouched down below the bar and, looking up at the ceiling, made the sign of a cross, touching his forehead, chest and two shoulders with his index finger. Ray picked up the first glass of whisky and downed it, he was now alone in the bar with the terrified barman who remained crouched down. Ray swallowed the second drink and then, gun still in hand, made his way out on to the street where people who had heard the gun shots and wanted to be nosey were now parting like the red sea at the sight of the armed hitman, leaving him with plenty of space around him, he looked left and right, Ray saw two figures that had picked up their pace and were the only two moving toward him, he noticed that they too were carrying guns. Ray stood his ground and waited for the two men to get closer, "Time this wrong and I'm fucked" he thought. Ray squeezed the trigger on his gun and the first geezer hit the deck, within a split second he squeezed again as the second one hesitated slightly and glanced down at the figure on the floor. Ray walked over to the two prone figures and buried one more bullet in each of them, he then put the gun back in his pocket before turning and walking away, in the distance he could hear police sirens and picked up his pace. By the time the cars screeched to a halt outside the boozer Ray was several streets away and out of harms way.

There was one last job for Ray, he needed to pay Claire a visit but it would have to be a bit lively because once she found out that Big H was no longer alive she would have a few more bodyguards by her side, the hit man was sure of that. Ray stopped a passing black cab and got in the back where he announced the address of the brothel to the driver and he was on his way.

Claire had sent two of her minders to help Big H remove Ray form the planet, she was waiting for news, hopefully the good sort and poured herself a large G and T. When the front door of the brothel opened and Ray walked in to the hallway her 'boat' was a picture, the shocked look of surprise mixed with fear caused Ray to laugh as he locked the door behind him.

"Surprised to see me? I'm not a ghost or a figment of your imagination," Ray laughed and then pinched himself, "Ouch! Definitely alive and that pinch just fuckin' hurt, anyway we have some unsettled business I think."

Claire couldn't speak for the moment but moved towards her counter where the alarm button was on the underside and her G & T was sitting on top, she had only just moved away from it and was pissed at her timing.

"Whoa! Stop there bitch, turn and come over here." Claire did as she was told, Ray grabbed her arm and walked her to her living room.

"Pour me a whisky and don't try anything stupid." Ray pulled the gun from his jacket pocket, "I don't wanna have to kill you yet 'cos I aint into fucking corpses."

The words excited Claire and her eyes lit up, Ray noticed the look and laughed as she handed him his drink, he closed the living room door and slid a chair under the handle, "We don't want anybody walking in and spoiling our fun do we?"

Claire didn't answer, she didn't have to, her eyes were giving away her thoughts. Ray lifted his gun and pointed it at her but he was pretty sure that it wasn't necessary, "Clothes off Claire, all of them."

The madam started with the buttons on her blouse, pulling it out from the black pencil skirt that she was wearing. She then undid her skirt and stepped out of it, the sight before Ray was exciting him, the brothel owner was standing there in her bra and knickers, suspenders and stockings, all black as were the high heels she was wearing, a small noise escaped Ray's lips and Claire smiled before looking down at his crutch, the bulge was clear and it was Claire's turn to make a small moan as she walked over to

Ray and unzipped his flies before putting her hand inside and, wrestling with his underpants, she pulled his erection free and gave it a gentle squeeze. Another moan escaped and Ray lifted the gun to Claire's head. "No funny business!" The statement was followed by a sigh as Claire started to massage his cock.

"Just fuck me Ray," Claire kicked off her shoes and coaxed her would-be rapist over to the sofa, "I want this as much as you."

It wasn't what Ray expected her to say and for a moment he was disappointed, Claire was looking at him and a small panic hit her, "Oh fuck! He wanted the thrill of the rape." She quickly dropped to her knees and ran her tongue the length of his erection before putting it in her mouth, Ray moaned with delight and the woman's panic ebbed away as she continued to work her magic on him and just before he wanted to orgasm Ray pulled her off and upright. Claire rubbed her tongue over her lips as Ray pushed her onto the sofa before undoing his trousers and stepping out of them and his pants, his gun was still pointed at Claire and this, for her, added to the pleasure, she slipped her knickers off and opened her legs, Ray accepted the invitation and a delightful little squeal left Claire's lips as he entered her, aware of the gun still pointing at her head the pleasure intensified for her and she had her first orgasm. The moistness ray felt pleased him and he thrust harder and faster, Claire was moving with him and then 'Boom!' they climaxed together.

Claire had had the second fuck she'd been dreaming of and Ray had satisfied his want too, both of them felt the need to lay in each other's arms and dream of happiness for a while and then together they realised that wasn't going to happen, it couldn't.

"You bastard" Claire screamed and pushed Ray off her. "You just raped me!" She started to slap her palms on his chest "Bastard, Bastard, Bastard" she screamed and then as she heard Ray pull back the hammer on his gun she began to cry.

"I could think of worse ways of leaving this life" she thought and squeezed her eyes shut and waited for it to all be over. She waited but it never happened and so she dared to open her 'minces' and sneak a peak, Ray was dressed and sitting on an armchair opposite the sofa. Claire closed her legs and sat up and then realised Ray was no longer holding the gun, the relief that flooded over her whole body caused her to fall back against the sofa and then she started crying, gently at first but that feeling of relief kept pouring out and then she was crying full on, Ray sat and watched, then it was like someone turned a switch off as she stopped and pulled herself upright. Anger replaced the self-pity as she realised that she'd orgasmed more than once during the sex with a man that had taken so much from her. Her expression changed as she stood up screaming that she hated the man sitting opposite.

"How can I take you serious when you're wearing what you are, you are one sexy woman Claire and that fuck, just like the first one, was better than good but will there be a third time? I don't think so!"

Claire looked at herself and wearing just a pair of stockings, suspenders and a bra, she had to admit that she was not dressed for a bull and cow and that angered her more.

She ran at Ray with both arms pumping like pistons, her clenched fists coming down with intention, Ray stood up and let several blows land before grabbing her wrists and pulling her close and then they were together and Claire planted a smacker straight on Ray's lips, he pulled her even closer and returned the kiss while letting go of her wrists, he wrestled with her bra strip and she started pulling at his clothes, and then that third fuck that he had just said would never happen did. The feelings he'd told himself he would never have again after his hapless affair with Brenda had just reappeared and Ray knew that he was once again thinking about compromising his future. The sex over, this time the pair lay on the carpet, both sighed but neither spoke, Claire cuddled up to Ray and started to draw circles on his chest with her finger, time seemed to stop and it appeared to have been forever before the madam broke the silence, "I should hate you ya bastard, so why don't I?" Claire stopped drawing the circles and lifted herself up above Ray. "Was that just sex, or more? I'm confused to fuck Ray." Straddling her supposed rapist she took hold of him again and a few rubs later she had what she wanted, Claire sat on his erection and moved up and down slowly, Ray took hold of her tits and started to massage them, Claire closed her eyes, moving faster and faster as Ray's squeeze intensified and once more the pair exploded as one, Claire collapsed on top of Ray, both were panting and then Claire whooped, "Wow! That was some fuck mister!" a giggle escaped her lips and the fully grown woman that she was had just become a teenager again. "Wow!" Claire followed the expression with a laugh and started planting kisses on Ray's neck, then she had his earlobe between her teeth and chewed gently, her fingers were caressing Ray's hair and he closed his eyes with the intensity of the pleasure that was sweeping through him. He was no longer a hit man and she no longer a brothel owner instead they were two love-struck teenagers exploring each others bodies with their hands and tongues, Ray was on top and Claire was moaning with delight as he ran his tongue over her and planted small kisses everywhere, then Claire was on top and it was Ray's turn to moan with delight and then they were fucking each other again. When it was over they were laying together once more when Ray brought them both back to the present. The lust, love, passion, care free spirit or whatever it was had to stop, they were in the here and now. "I killed Big H earlier Claire and the two mugs with him."

Claire sat up and looked at him, "I guessed that you bastard, now I hate you, hate you, hate you" She stood up and collected her dress and put it on, "Get dressed and get the fuck out of here."

"But where do we…" Ray started.

"We don't, we fuckin' don't Ray, we just don't."

The crying continued and so Ray got dressed and left the brothel.

"I will kill you or have you killed Ray, I promise."

Ray did not hear the threat from Claire but as he left the brothel he sighed heavily. The sex had been intense and the affair brief, he knew the two of them could never be an item but he was now left wondering whether he should have added her to his list of victims. It could prove dangerous for him letting her live. Sometimes life was shit, Ray pulled up the collar on his jacket against the cold and walked away. Claire relived the sex she'd just had and smiled, she wondered for a moment if life with Ray would work, it was a short-lived thought before she turned her thoughts to fulfilling the promise she had just made.

When DCI Joe Brown received the call, he was less than impressed to hear that there were four more corpses on his patch. It shook him up a bit when he arrived at the scene, a boozer in London in the middle of the day to find two heavies on the pavement with two bullets apiece buried in them but it was the discovery of Big H inside that shook him to the core.

"Thank fuck I'm in a boozer", the copper took out his packet of cigarettes and lit one up, he inhaled the smoke and then blew it out, "cos right now I need a double bloody whisky."

GLOSSARY

Adam And Eve .... Believe

Beak .... Nose

Belly Up .... Wrong

Bit Of Skirt .... Woman

Boat Race .... Face

Boat .... Face

Bonce .... Head

Bull and Cow .... Row

Carzy .... Toilet

Claret .... Blood

Gaff .... Home

Geezer .... Man

Half Inching .... Stealing

Kip .... Sleep

Kisser .... Face

Mars Bar .... Scar

Mince Pies .... Eyes

Minces .... Eyes

Mug .... Fool Idiot

Nick .... Steal

Pop Him .... Shoot Him

Quick Shifty .... Quick Look

Ruby Murray .... Curry

Scooby Doo .... Clue

Scooby .... Clue

Shanks's Pony .... Walking

Shut Eye .... Sleep

Tea Leaf .... Thief

Tom Foolery .... Jewellery

Trouble and Strife ...... Wife

Wedge .... Money

Wedge .... Payment

Whistle and Flute .... Suit

Whistle .... Suit

ACKNOWLEDGEMENTS

Many thanks to Sue, Muriel, Deb and to the little man that lives inside my head and helps me to create the characters and build the plot.

About the Author

William Ernest Palmer (Bill) currently lives on the Costa Blanca in Spain.

Bill was born in Kentish Town, North West London in 1957, the sixth of eight children and the first son. His parents moved the family to Letchworth Garden City when Bill was seven years old where he lived until moving to Spain in 2002.

Bill boxed for the Hitchin Youth Boxing Club and for whom his first contest was on November the 14th 1968. He continued to box for the club proving victorious in sixty of seventy-five contests, winning a National Schoolboy Title and boxing for England along the way.

Bill has been a builder for most of his life, and worked as a doorman and minder for several years. Meeting and mixing with a variety of people from many walks of life one boss once described Bill as a society misfit saying, "you look and sound like you drink lager and frequent football terraces, but you are in fact an educated man." Bill passed the 11+ exam and went to Grammar School.

Now Bill is approaching 64 years of age he hopes to become a full time writer after 48 years in the building trade.

Printed in Great Britain
by Amazon